STRAW BOSS SHOWDOWN

Whitey stepped around the fire and advanced on Billy Joe. He licked his lips. This wasn't going to be much of a fight. He'd take the kid and jerk him up and snap him over his knee like a stick of dry firewood and that would be it.

Billy Joe stood and watched him come and when the distance was right his left hand snaked out and flattened the nose of the straw boss. It was a shock to Whitey. Not the pain, but the suddenness of it. He felt blood on his upper lip and he heard a mutter from the drovers.

He grabbed for the slender cowboy but his hands came away empty. Then a streaking right fist collided with his cheekbone and his head rocked back on his thick neck.

It wasn't supposed to work this way. In the light of the campfire, Whitey's face was a terrible crimson. He moved forward, and when Billy Joe stepped to one side, the straw boss was ready. A big hand closed on his upper shoulder and Billy Joe knew there was trouble breathing in his ear.

Bantam Books by W. W. Southard

BITTER PECOS
A RECKONING AT ARROWHEAD

BITTER PECOS

W. W. Southard

BANTAM BOOKS
TORONTO · NEW YORK · LONDON · SYDNEY

BITTER PECOS
A Bantam Book / May 1984

ISBN 0-553-24236-9

Published simultaneously in the United States and Canada

Bantam Books are published by Bantam Books, Inc. Its trade-
mark, consisting of the words ''Bantam Books'' and the por-
trayal of a rooster, is Registered in U.S. Patent and Trademark
Office and in other countries. Marca Registrada. Bantam
Books, Inc., 666 Fifth Avenue, New York, New York 10103.

PRINTED IN THE UNITED STATES OF AMERICA

O   0 9 8 7 6 5 4 3 2 1

To Dad and Mother

Chapter One

Billy Joe Chance came on the men unexpectedly. They were gathered on their horses in a semicircle under a lone grove of cottonwood trees in a barren ocean of prairie. Even from a quarter-mile away he could feel a hair-trigger tension in the air, air as still as the inside of a pitch-black cellar.

Beyond the cottonwoods was the herd of longhorns, but they weren't moving. They were waiting for whatever was happening in the heavy shade under the canopy of trees.

Chance felt the tension again, thick enough to cut with a jackknife. Beneath the trees a dozen drovers, silent and unsmiling, sat their horses. It was not until Billy Joe drew close that he saw the object of their attention.

At the center of the tautly drawn circle of horsemen was an emigrant wagon, with a man and a woman seated side by side on the high, wooden seat. The bearded driver had the look of a man anxious to get his team of oxen moving.

But his way was blocked by a tall, blue roan horse on which sat a lean, weathered cowboy.

Chance looked him over. It didn't take any special talent to figure that he was the boss of the outfit. He was hewn from that kind of timber.

No one looked Billy Joe's way when he rode up. They were listening with uneasy intensity to the exchange between the cowboy on the blue roan and the lean, stooped man with the beard and squinting eyes who sat on the wagon seat.

"I told you. You ain't going anywhere until I get a look in that wagon," said the trail boss. The words weren't loud, or angry, but they had the unforgiving ring of an ax blade against an oak stump.

"You'll play the devil," the old man said. "Get outta my way or I'll lay this here whip acrost yore back. They ain't nobody gonna search my wagon. You hear?"

The woman on the seat beside the old man had the same dry, pinched countenance, shriveled by too many years and too much sun and wind, like the wrinkled skin of a last year's apple.

"Go ahead and lay one acrost him, Silas," she urged the old man.

And Silas did. He swung the long bullwhip in a hissing arc toward the head and shoulders of the horseman. But the length of braided leather found a low-hanging cottonwood limb and entwined itself about the branch.

The trail boss reached out a hand and jerked the bullwhip from the old man's grasp.

"A couple of you boys empty that wagon. Dump it out on the ground. Everything."

He pointed with the stock of the whip toward the couple on the wagon seat. The words were not directed to anyone in particular.

"Keep an eye on them two."

He and the three drovers didn't have far to look. The pile of household goods—shabby things, mostly worn beyond redemption—had not grown very large before Chance heard the big man utter an oath. A moment later he came from behind the wagon carrying a rolled-up steerhide.

"Get 'em down here," he commanded.

A drover moved in and gestured with his hand. Wearing a look of defiant guilt, the old man began climbing down from his high perch. Another puncher stepped up to the wheel and offered a hand to the old woman.

"Get yore hands off'n me, you no-good hooligan," she snapped.

The puncher backed away and let her climb down by herself.

The trail boss made a production of it. He took one end of the rolled-up hide and flipped it out, hair side up. The mottled brown-and-white hide spread to its full length and he let it settle to the ground. Except for the buzzing of a handful of bottle flies, the silence was complete. Not a man spoke. The brands on the hide were as clear as the sun that burned down on the prairie and set waves of light to dancing on the distant horizon.

The bearded oldster and the woman with the bonnet half-covering her face just stood there side by side and looked down at the hide. Finally, he looked up and spat a stream of brown into the grass a hand's breadth from the spurred boot of his accuser.

"Wal," he grunted. "What're you gonna do about it?"

"I'm gonna fix it so you don't steal no more beef from my herd," said the trail boss without emotion. He waved his hand in a quick arc to the cowboys standing on the ground. "Take hold of him, boys."

Then the big puncher stepped to the side of his mount, took down the horsehair rope coiled at the swell, and deliberately began to shake out a small loop. Astride his horse at the outer edge of the circle, Billy Joe Chance felt the hair lifting along the back of his neck.

The trail boss passed the loop over the old man's head, knocking his shapeless hat to the ground. The old man's seamed, brown face was in startling contrast to the rim of white that banded his forehead. Wisps of thin, gray hair were plastered to his head by perspiration.

"Get my horse," said the tall, grim-faced drover.

A cowboy caught the reins of the blue roan and led him forward. The trail boss nodded to the two punchers standing beside the old man. They each took an elbow and moved forward.

Holding his head tilted to one side so the knot of the horsehair rope beneath his ear wouldn't scratch, the old man spat again. This time his aim was true. The stream of brown juice splattered against the high top of the big man's boot and ran down across the instep.

The trail boss grunted an oath and jerked the noose

tighter about the scrawny, wrinkled neck. The old man turned and looked for a long moment at his wife. Neither said a word. Then the two cowboys lifted him into the saddle on the long roan.

It was no more than a dozen steps to the big limb of the cottonwood. The trail boss tossed up the coils of rope, missed, and tossed them up again. Then he caught the knotted end of the long lariat and tied it around the big, rough trunk of the tree.

The old man with the graying beard sat in the expensive, hand-tooled saddle and looked down at the trail boss.

"You wuthless Texan son of a bitch," he said.

Billy Joe saw the old man's Adam's apple jerk as he swallowed the tobacco juice in his mouth. He also saw in the pale, narrowed eyes a sudden realization that it wasn't going to stop, that this wasn't to be just a foolish little drama to serve as a warning.

Then, without ceremony, the big man slapped the rump of the roan. The horse leaped forward. The old man's eyes grew large. He reached up and clawed at the taut rope with both hands. His feet ran frantically, vainly seeking a solid purchase. Wetness oozed down a trouser leg, streaking the dark, dust-crusted fabric.

The old woman lurched back against the wagon wheel and caught at it for support. She bit her lower lip, making no sound.

Billy Joe watched without expression. But a chill, like the cold belly of a snake, lay against his spine. He was remembering another hanging, another time when he'd watched a man's body jerk at the end of a rope.

Chapter Two

Before the old man's body had stopped its convulsive twitching, the drovers were pulling away, heading back toward the herd. Chance rode in beside a lone puncher on a stocking-legged sorrel.

"Who's the boss of this outfit?"

The other man studied him for a long moment from the deep shadows beneath the brim of his hat.

"Who wants to know?"

Billy Joe considered his reply. The puncher's attitude was something less than cordial. Finally, he said, "I'm looking to hire on."

The other man drew his horse to a halt.

"His name's Gideon Stroop. But don't bother to ask. We don't need any more hands."

Chance looked at him evenly.

"If it's all the same, I'll do my own askin' of him."

The other cowboy shoved his hat to the back of his head. Beneath an overhang of chalky white eyebrows, his eyes were a washed-out blue. They reminded Billy Joe of the faded eyes of the old woman under the cottonwood trees.

"You're talkin' to the straw boss of this outfit right now. And I'm tellin' you we don't need any more hands," said the man with the pale eyes. "If you're lookin' for a handout, go get some grub from Solomon over at the chuck wagon. Otherwise, just drift on out."

Billy Joe regarded him silently. Finally, he said, "Thanks, anyway."

Then he reined his horse about and rode west, toward the point of the herd. He could feel the pale eyes of the straw boss on his back.

The trail boss was already there, sitting his long-legged blue roan on a halfhearted ridge of barren ground and watching the tide of longhorns begin to shift into motion below him.

Chance reined in beside him.

"Your straw boss said the outfit didn't need any more hands. Thought I'd better ask you."

Gideon Stroop didn't even look at him. His eyes were scanning the herd.

"He told you right."

Billy Joe sat silently for a long moment, his eyes,

too, on the herd, beginning to move westward in a trickle, like a pool of water finding a low point through which to slide away.

"The way I figure it, you'll need another hand."

Stroop jerked his eyes from the herd and for the first time looked at Chance.

"What'd you say?"

"You're gonna need another puncher. For a few days, anyway."

The trail boss's gaze wasn't friendly.

"Well, now. You just go on and tell me why I need another hand."

Billy Joe met his gaze.

"You've got to send somebody back to Fort Picket with that old woman."

Stroop looked at him long and coldly. It was as if this upstart kid had read his mind.

At last he said, "That's her problem."

"I suppose you saw the Comanche sign a day or two back," said Chance.

"They brought it on themselves," said Stroop. "Damned old hardhead knew better. I'd already warned him once."

Billy Joe regarded him steadily, without speaking. The silence grew long. Stroop shifted uneasily in his saddle. Finally he looked at Chance.

"You know anything about trail drivin'?"

"Some," said Billy Joe.

"You been up the trail, I guess."

Billy Joe nodded.

"Been up the Abilene trail a couple of times. And made the Hunnewell drive."

The trail boss obviously didn't like it but he was out on a long, thin limb.

He swore under his breath and pointed back toward the far end of the herd.

"Go find Whitey and tell him to send the Mex back with the old woman."

"Whitey the gent with the washed-out hair and the disposition of a prickly pear?"

"That's him." Stroop nodded.

Billy Joe reined the dun horse about.

"What's your handle?" asked the trail boss.

"Much obliged for the job," said Chance, and gigged his horse into a sudden run. He didn't look back but he knew Gideon Stroop was following his departure with a hard gaze.

Whitey's countenance held no warmth when Billy Joe rode up.

"You don't listen so good," he grunted. "Like I said, we don't need no more hands."

Billy Joe pushed back his hat and surveyed the straw boss with a long, slow gaze. His eyes wandered over the shag of chalk-white hair escaping from around his hat, and similar patches of sun-bleached growth over his eyes and along his upper lip. The flesh of his face was pale and lifeless, except where the sun had reached under the big brim of his hat and touched his nose and his chin. Those places were a bright red, as though he'd stood too long too close to a red-hot stove.

By the time Billy Joe had finished his silent appraisal, there was crimson in the face of the straw boss that couldn't be laid to the heat of the sun.

"You're wasting my valuable time," he said. "I'll tell you the same thing Stroop told you. Hit the trail back to wherever you came from."

Chance let the hint of a grin pull at his mouth.

"He must've changed his mind without conferrin' with you, Whitey. He wants you to send the Mex to ride back to Fort Picket with the old woman. I'll be takin' his place."

Whitey's jaws came together with an audible snap.

"The hell you say!" he snorted. "We'll see about that."

He kicked the sorrel horse into motion with a force that brought a grunt from the animal. Billy Joe watched him disappear in a boiling cloud of dust in the direction of the point. The grin on his face tightened. Whitey wasn't the kind of man to forget a bit of ignominy, especially that served to him by a brand-new hired hand.

Chance didn't wait for the straw boss's return but reined about and headed toward the drag, the twitching tail of the serpentine herd where a thick curtain of alkali dust was ribboning toward the azure of the Texas sky, where a trio of turkey buzzards balanced effortlessly in a thermal from the prairie floor. The drag was where the greenhorns and the humble and those not in favor would be found. That was where the Mex would be riding.

The brightly burnished orange of the late afternoon sun was fooling around with the dusky violet of the horizon when Billy Joe saw Stroop, a speck in the distance, stand in his stirrups and wave his hat in a circle over his head. It was time to ease off, to drift the longhorns into a loose circle, to let them find what grazing they could before they bedded down for the night.

Billy Joe unknotted the kerchief that covered his mouth and nose, wiped the stiff icing of dust from around his eyes, and loped in toward the remuda bunched a distance from the chuck wagon. The horse wrangler was a short, skinny youth with a patch of fuzz under his nose that he hoped would be mistaken for a mustache. It could be, until the dirt was washed from it.

He was throwing up an enclosure fashioned from horsehair ropes when Chance rode up.

"Say," said the horse wrangler. "I ain't seen you before, have I?"

"Nope."

"My name's Maples. They call me Runt."

Billy Joe nodded and went on unsaddling the sweat-caked dun horse.

"You ridin' with the herd? You ridin' all the way to Fort Sumner?" inquired the youth.

"Maybe."

"I've done plenty of punchin'," said Runt. "Mr. Stroop's gonna let me be a drover soon's he finds somebody else to wrangle these ol' ponies. That's what he told me."

"That's fine," said Billy Joe.

"Got my own saddle and everything. See?" The youth pointed to a piebald horse ground-tied a few steps away. On the back of the spotted pony was an ancient rimfire saddle, its stirrup fenders dried and cracked and the leather ties chewed off short by an inquisitive calf in the corral of some careless, long-past owner.

Billy Joe solemnly inspected the saddle and just as solemnly nodded his approval.

"First one I've ever owned," said Maples. "Bought it 'fore we pulled out from the Brazos."

Billy Joe started away toward the chuck wagon.

"Hey, you never did tell me your name," called Maples.

Chance didn't look back.

A dozen or more drovers were scattered on their haunches in a semicircle around the campfire, washing down beef and beans and sourdough biscuits with a bitter, scalding liquid the cook swore was as good as any coffee east of the Continental Divide.

Gideon Stroop stood beside the chuck wagon with a foot cocked up on the hub of a wheel, rolling a cigarette. He stooped, took a burning splinter from the coals, and fired the cigarette hanging from his lips. Through a curl of blue smoke he watched Billy Joe approach.

After a time, he tossed the burning stick aside and returned to his post beside the wagon wheel. The rattle of conversation among the drovers had ceased as Billy Joe walked into the circle of the fire's illumination.

Then Stroop spoke.

"This here gent is ridin' with us until Julio gets back from Fort Picket. Claims he's seen the rear end of a few longhorns headin' up the trail to Abilene."

A couple of punchers nodded. The others mostly poked around at what was left on their tin plates. Billy Joe wondered at the lack of cordiality. Then he heard a rasping voice from the rim of the firelight and his wondering came to an end. The voice was that of the straw boss.

"It's a helluva note when a herd can't get by for three or four days being one man short, and that man a greaser,

to boot. Guess we'll hire on every saddle bum we run
across from here to the Pecos River.''

It was as much a disparagement of Gideon Stroop as
it was of Billy Joe but the trail boss offered no comment.
Instead, he took the cigarette from his mouth, blew the
ashes from the tip, and studied the glowing stub. Chance
saw it then. Whatever opinion the straw boss might feel
compelled to express about Stroop's handling of the crew
or the herd, he was free to express it.

In the silence that followed Whitey's words, Billy Joe
secured a tin cup and lifted the blackened coffeepot from
the bed of coals.

''Yeah,'' he said, pouring the steaming black liquid
into the cup. ''And some outfits hire them saddle bums
before they ever start a drive.''

He looked up then and saw Whitey getting quickly to
his feet. Even in the shadows at the far edge of the
firelight, the red in Whitey's face was apparent. Billy Joe
carefully replaced the coffeepot, regained his feet, and
sipped at the coffee. Over the rim of the cup, his eyes were
on the straw boss.

Whitey handed his plate to another puncher and
wiped his hands on his chaps.

''So you've been to Abilene a time or two, have you?
Well, it won't come as no surprise to an old hand like
yourself that somebody's gotta ride night herd.'' He stood
on spread feet and hooked his thumbs in his gun belt.
''Now, go catch you up a fresh hoss and get out there and
keep them longhorns company.''

Billy Joe looked at the straw boss for the space of a
deep breath. Then he turned up the cup, poured the coffee
into the dust, and tossed the cup across the campfire to
Whitey. Instinctively, the straw boss reached out to catch
it. Billy Joe didn't wait. He turned and strode away, back
toward the remuda.

A dozen steps into the semidarkness he met Runt
Maples, headed for the chuck wagon with his old saddle
over one shoulder.

''Say,'' said the youth, ''you're some fast eater.''

Billy Joe grinned in the half-light.

"That straw boss of yours thought I ought to work up an appetite first. I need a horse."

"Catch up that blaze-faced black if you can see him in the dark. He's as good a night horse as there is in the bunch."

"Much obliged," said Billy Joe.

"Sure thing, Abilene," said the boy, and walked on toward the campfire.

For half a moment Billy Joe stood and wondered at the name the wrangler had used, then remembered what Whitey had said. Well, mused Billy Joe, he'd been called worse things than Abilene.

The blaze-faced black was hell to catch and worse to saddle and Billy Joe thought he would have his hands full when he straddled the long-legged gelding. But the horse only halfheartedly humped his back, then broke into a lope at the touch of the spurs.

Another rider loomed out of the darkness. Billy Joe reined up.

"I'm supposed to relieve somebody," he said.

"Yeah, me." The other puncher thumbed back his hat and Chance saw a seamed, weathered face over a ragged, gray mustache.

"You're the new one, I reckon, but I won't argue at anybody that wants to take my place wet-nursin' these damn ladinos."

He spat tobacco juice from the cud in his cheek. Billy Joe heard it splatter.

"What do they call you when it's time to eat?" the grizzled puncher asked.

"Well, that sawed-off horse wrangler didn't need an introduction. He sort of took a fancy to 'Abilene,'" said Chance.

The other man chuckled.

"That kid's plumb got it figured out," he said. "He'll be a trail boss one of these days."

When Billy Joe didn't reply, he went on.

"My name's Smith. Arlo Smith. Believe it or don't, that's the handle I was born with." He chuckled again, as though enjoying a joke he'd considered a hundred times before. "You'd be surprised how many relations I've run across out here in Texas. But most of 'em weren't born with the name. It was just handy when they was lookin' to shake somebody off their trail."

Abruptly, like the twitching tail of a cat, a cool breeze flicked them in the face and was gone. In the distance, along the western horizon, Billy Joe saw a sudden play of lightning and heard a muttering of thunder.

"How many we got on night herd?" he asked.

"Four," said Arlo Smith. "You and three others. That gives you about eight hundred head of longhorns apiece to keep pacified."

"I don't like the smell of it," said Chance. "Looks like a good night for a run."

"A stampede? Well, I ain't seen any sign of one. These old steers look plenty happy to get off their feet."

But the longhorns were restless. Billy Joe could feel it hanging heavily in the night air. There was more rattling of horns than there should have been. Eerie splashes of green fire lanced here and there among the horn tips.

"Just the same, you might tell Stroop. Wouldn't hurt to have the boys keep a horse saddled."

Arlo Smith and his mount faded into the dimness in the direction of the chuck wagon. Billy Joe had taken a liking to the older cowboy, but he still didn't like the sharp, wild scent that stung his nostrils. He'd smelled it before, when a herd of longhorns was getting itself worked up to break.

But nothing happened. The steers milled some, got up and turned around and lay back down, all except an old, knife-backed steer the color of a fish's belly. He roamed the outer edge of the herd, rattling a warning deep in his throat and hooking at anything in his way.

The other night herders stood their two-hour shifts and were relieved, but no one showed up to take Billy Joe's place. He grunted to himself. That would be the work of the straw boss. Whitey would take some pleasure in leaving him on night guard for a few extra turns.

It was sometime after midnight, Chance judged, when they broke. The patches of lightning and thunder that had held their threatening conversations on the distant horizon had moved in closer. The breeze had stopped. It was dead quiet except for a continual celestial muttering, like a growling in the empty belly of a hungry giant.

Another rider, silhouetted by the intermittent flashes of lightning, drew near.

"Who's there?" asked the thin voice of Runt Maples.

"Abilene," replied Billy Joe.

"Hey," said the youth. "How come you're still out here? Everybody else pulls a two-hour trick."

"Ol' Whitey's just taken a liking to me, I guess," said Chance.

"Well, that don't rightly seem fair," said Maples.

"Fair's what the boss says is fair," grunted Chance.

He waved his hand in a half-circle, and in the sudden illumination from a jagged bolt of lightning his arm took on the spectral quality of a bat in startled flight.

"I've got a feeling about this bunch of longhorns, Runt. I'd wager we see a stampede before we see daylight."

Maples's tone surprised him. It wasn't filled with fear and awe at the idea of more than three thousand stampeding longhorns. Rather, the youth sounded half-eager with excitement.

"You think so, Abilene? You really think so? Shoot, I ain't never been close to a stampede. That oughta be somethin' to write home about."

In the darkness, Chance shook his head at the recklessness of boyhood. Had he ever been so full of idiocy?

"Listen, kid." He made his voice hard. "You don't want to see these outlaws in an all-out run across this prairie at night. But let me give you a little advice. If they do start to run, you get on the left side of the herd. The only way to stop a run is to get 'em milling to the right. And a man sure don't want to get caught in the middle. Hear?"

"Sure, Abilene," said the Runt. "I savvy. But they probably won't be tearin' loose tonight. I got a feel about it."

They separated then, the kid moving on in one direction, Chance drifting away in the other.

When it began he heard no warning sound, felt no change in the atmosphere. In an instant, thirty-two hundred longhorn steers took leave of their senses, sprang to their feet, and swept away into the darkness in a terror-stricken, mindless run.

Chapter Three

The black horse with the blaze face was everything the wrangler had claimed, and more. He ran hell-for-leather with the stampeding herd, but he ran with confidence and authority. It could have been a noonday sun under which he ran, rather than a patchwork of black shadows that could hold any form of peril.

Billy Joe nonetheless rode with his toes light in the stirrups, expecting at any moment to feel the black fall away beneath him. But he held the racing horse in close to the raging longhorn tide, crowding in to start the mill that would bring them to a grudging halt.

The booming thunder from the heavens merged with the thunder of twelve thousand pounding hooves to create one immense, paralyzing roar. The herd had, by a stroke of good fortune, begun its run in a northerly direction, away from the chuck wagon and the sleeping drovers.

The eeriness of it raised the hair along the back of Billy Joe's neck. There were no sounds of laboring or terror, no bawling from the stampeding brutes; only the drum of their hooves and the crackling of horns that clashed like dueling swords in the darkness. And when they did come together, splashes of green fire punctured the blackness like pelting drops of rain driving against the mirror stillness of a pool of water.

There was no sign of the other night guards. Billy Joe knew he was nearer the point of the running herd than the others. He had passed them all as he quietly circled the herd a short time before his conversation with Runt Maples.

Maples! He wondered abruptly where the kid was now. Somewhere behind him, he supposed, quirting his racing horse beside the crashing tide of longhorn cattle and shouting into the wind to shore up his courage. But the youth wouldn't likely again express such foolishness as he had a few minutes ago. Riding the riptide of a stampede was like going to war. Anticipation could set a man's belly on fire with fear-shot eagerness. But when the maiming and killing started, the sport became suddenly less thrilling.

Chance reined the black horse tight against the running cattle, crowding them toward the right, toward a milling spiral that would force a halt to their flight. But the longhorns were blinded by the mindlessness of their own frenzy. He pulled his six-gun and fired into the ground at the very ear of a big brindle steer. The tide of running beef kept running, and he fired again.

Almost as an echo he heard another shot, a faint report somewhere behind him. Then the cattle began a gradual swing away from him and he pushed them harder. The mill had started.

It was the better part of an hour, Chance judged, before the crazed longhorns had packed themselves into such a whirlpool of rattling horns and pounding hooves that running was impossible. But the mill had broken the stampede.

Now the noise began. Now he could hear the wheeze of panting steers, hear them gasping for air, hear them bawling for their running mates. Their restlessness kept them on their feet, but the running was out of them for this night.

"Damn bunch of lunatic critters," muttered a voice from the darkness. "I swear they're worse'n a bunch of weak-minded sheep."

The horse and rider moved closer. Chance saw the outline of a puncher's head and shoulders. The man was hatless.

"Say, ain't you the new hand? The one they call Abilene?" asked the rider.

"Yeah."

"Well, looks like you got 'em turned."

"Where's the rest of the boys?" asked Billy Joe.

"Beats me," said the cowboy. "I still had my horse saddled when they started. But the rest of 'em were in their bedrolls. They're back yonder somewhere, I guess. I figure we run five miles or better."

He swore again, going into some detail on the ancestry of longhorns, individually and collectively.

"And on top of all that, I lost my damn hat."

"Was that you that fired the shot a little ways back?" asked Billy Joe.

"Nope, not me. I heard a couple of shots from your direction and I thought I heard another gun go off somewhere. But there wasn't no way of tellin' where it came from."

Chance shifted in his saddle, seeking a comfortable posture and finding none. He'd been glued to that bit of buckstitched leather for twenty hours. It was beginning to tell.

"Well, it's you and me then, pardner. We've got three, maybe four, hours till daylight."

"If we're gonna start keeping company, you can call me Leroy," said the other.

The steers made no further attempt to run, and at last Chance saw a band of gray etch an outline of the eastern horizon. As soon as it was light enough to tell which end of the steer wore the horns, they began hazing the herd southward.

Billy Joe saw it first. It was a lump of blackness in a landscape turning gray and he supposed it to be a clump of bear grass that the herd had beaten down as it thundered along its insane path. But a few more paces and another handful of daylight showed him it wasn't bear grass. It was a saddle—or what had been a saddle.

He reined up the black horse, stepped down, and turned it over with the toe of his boot. It was the cracked, ancient saddle he'd seen the evening before. The saddle

Runt Maples had displayed with unabashed pride. The first one he had owned.

"Aw, hell," said Billy Joe Chance.

He stood there in the semidarkness with the saddle at his feet and the longhorns swinging past a few yards away and built himself a cigarette. He wasn't in any hurry to locate the owner of that saddle.

"Head 'em over that way." He waved a hand in Leroy's direction and the cowboy veered the herd away.

Billy Joe mounted and rode on while the bright pink in the east fused into orange. He hadn't ridden fifty yards when he found Runt Maples. The wrangler who had wanted worse than anything in the world to become a drover had paid the price of being one. He was lying face down. He was smeared with prairie soil and his clothes were in ribbons.

Chance knelt and rolled him over onto his back. There wasn't much to look at where his face had been. Billy Joe took down his slicker, wrapped it about the body, and gently eased the boy across the rump of the edgy black horse.

"You made it, Runt," Billy Joe said half-aloud. "You made a cowhand, pardner."

With the coming of daylight, other drovers began to show up. Gideon Stroop was among the first. His face was bleak.

"Who is it?" he asked, nodding to the slicker-wrapped body behind Chance's saddle.

"Maples."

Stroop leaned an elbow on his saddle horn and looked off into the distance for a long while. Finally, he turned back.

"What set 'em off?"

"Can't say," replied Billy Joe. "They just took a notion to run."

Stroop swore, but without enthusiasm.

"We've got seventy miles of dry drivin' before we reach the Pecos. A stampede was just what we needed."

He started to ride on, then stopped.

"Too bad about the kid."

"Yeah," said Billy Joe. "Too bad about him."

Chance and Leroy rode side by side back to the chuck wagon, the silence lying heavily between them. Billy Joe laid the body of Runt Maples in the shade. Then he got a shovel and walked to the crest of a gentle knoll not far away and dug a grave. The ground was hard and dry. The buffalo grass that grew on its surface was surviving on fortitude. There wasn't any moisture to help it.

The weary herd reached them a little before noon. The cook, Solomon, located the Bible in the chuck wagon and Stroop read Psalm 23 while seventeen drovers stood mutely by with their hats in their hands. Then they buried the boy who had thought he was a man.

Stroop ordered the gaunt, weary herd held there for the remainder of the day. At sundown, the cook bellowed his signal to eat and the punchers moved toward the chuck wagon.

As before, Whitey took his plate and drifted out where the fringe of faint light from the campfire barely reached him. After a time, he looked beyond the fire where Billy Joe was sitting cross-legged, finishing his meal.

"I wanna know what happened to that herd last night. What caused 'em to set in to runnin'?"

Billy Joe went on about his eating as though Whitey's voice were only a waft of wind.

"You. Abilene." The straw boss's voice was sharply louder. "You was on night guard. How did them steers come to stampede?"

Chance fixed him with a steady gaze.

"Aw, you know how those old longhorns are. You can talk to 'em until you're blue in the face and they won't give you a straight answer."

Instantly the crimson spread across Whitey's face.

"Sort of like the answer you're givin' me now?"

"Sort of," said Chance.

Carefully, Whitey set his plate down and got to his feet. Billy Joe ignored the man and sat where he was, finishing the beans in the tin balanced on his lap.

"Abilene." Whitey's voice came to him low and cold across the short distance. "I ain't overly fond of you and that smart mouth of yours. Maybe you and me ought to come to an understanding.''

Billy Joe took the last bite, washed it down with a swallow of coffee, and stood.

''Anytime, Mr. Straw Boss,'' he said.

Almost as one man the dozen or more cowboys who had been seated cross-legged on the ground around the fire disengaged themselves from tin plates and coffee cups and drifted back into the shadows. None had a particular desire to do anything to hinder the flight of a stray bullet.

But Gideon Stroop, who had been leaning against the chuck wagon while he listened to the two men exchange pleasantries, now broke the quiet.

''You'll do it without guns if you do it. I won't have any man givin' them longhorns another excuse to stampede.''

Chance stood easy and relaxed, or so it seemed to the onlookers, but he made no move to shed his six-gun. At the end of a brief interval as taut as a banjo string, Whitey reached down, unbuckled his gun belt, and tossed it to a puncher standing a few paces away. Billy Joe followed suit.

Here and there, a drover glanced across the fire at another pair of eyes and nodded ever so slightly. There would be a great deal more entertainment in a fistfight between these two than in an argument settled with exploding power. Gunfights were messy, they were over almost as soon as they had begun, and more often than not the damage that resulted was of a permanent nature.

A cowboy called Mule Hunnicutt moved back into the shadows until he was standing beside the gray-mustachioed puncher named Arlo Smith. While both kept their eyes on the two combatants, Hunnicutt spoke quietly.

''Wanna put a few bucks on it?'' he asked.

''Why not?'' replied Arlo Smith. ''How you wanna make it?''

''I'll lay twenty in Yankee dollars that Whitey chews him up and spits him out quicker'n you can unsaddle a horse.''

''Even money?''

''Sure.''

"Well, now," said Arlo Smith. "You look at that there straw boss. He's as broad across the shoulders as a doubletree. And look at the size of his hands. A couple of hams, if ever I seen 'em."

He scrubbed at the stubble on his jaw.

"And you take a look at the kid. Skinny as a dogie calf. Why, he don't hardly weigh enough to leave tracks in a mudhole." He squinted from beneath the broad brim of his hat into the eyes of Hunnicutt. "You give me two to one and I'll cover that twenty-dollar bill. But you're stealin' my money."

Mule Hunnicutt concealed his grin with the back of a hand. It would be an easy ten dollars he was fixing to pilfer from the pocket of the old-timer.

Over the half-dozen steps that separated them, Billy Joe measured the straw boss. The man wasn't tall, probably not as tall as Billy Joe by three or four inches. But his build had the solid, unyielding ruggedness of a granite boulder. His neck was what they called a bull neck—short, and thick as the stump of a tree. His head sat directly on his shoulders without benefit of an extension.

And what shoulders they were. The fabric of his shirt had already, in a place or two, given way to the swell of brawn and sinew. He was doing it now, flexing his biceps at the pleasurable thought of getting his hands on this smart-mouth cowboy who had caused him nothing but grief since the first instant of their acquaintance.

The thought of what he had in mind brought a smile to Whitey's thin lips. He hadn't whipped any member of the crew since the fight on the day they'd pulled out from the Concho. No one had needed a second lesson. Now he was going to have another opportunity to demonstrate why it was unwise, unpleasant, and unhealthy to disagree with the straw boss—the man who rightfully should be trail boss of the whole lash-up.

Whitey stepped around the fire and advanced on the tall, slender cowboy. He licked his lips. This wasn't going to be much of a fight. He'd take the kid and jerk him up and snap him over his knee like a stick of dry firewood and that would be it.

Billy Joe stood and watched him come and when the distance was right his left hand snaked out and flattened the nose of the straw boss. It was a shock to Whitey. Not the pain, but the suddenness of it. He felt blood on his upper lip and he heard a mutter from the drovers.

He grabbed for the slender cowboy but his hands came away empty. Then a streaking right fist collided with his cheekbone and his head rocked back on his thick neck.

It wasn't supposed to work this way. In the light of the campfire, Whitey's face was a terrible crimson. He moved forward, and when Billy Joe stepped to one side, the straw boss was ready. A big hand closed on his upper shoulder and Billy Joe knew there was trouble breathing in his ear.

He tried to spin away but the hand closed tighter and Chance felt his flesh go numb to the tips of his fingers. If those huge arms ever got the hold they were seeking, his goose was cooked to a turn.

Three times Billy Joe drove a straight left fist into the face of the straw boss and three times Whitey only ducked his head and drew him closer.

The struggling pair shifted and parried and swayed over the campfire. Solomon, his small bird's eyes shining with pleasure, ducked in to save his coffeepot, suspended from the iron rod above the fire. He started to back up, then as an afterthought tossed a couple of mesquite roots onto the dying fire. There wasn't any use missing a good fight just because the light was bad.

Whitey's arms, arms as big around as a man's thigh might be, had found the hold they wanted. Billy Joe's own arms were pinioned against his sides by those bands of steel and Whitey was forcing him down, bending him backward until his knees had to buckle.

Billy Joe's head was the only thing that could move, and he moved it. He slammed the top of his head against the grimacing mouth of the straw boss. Chance felt the teeth sink into his scalp but he also felt the big arms relax their hold for an instant.

It was all he needed. He threw up his elbows and Whitey had to surrender his hold.

Billy Joe drove his right fist into the pit of Whitey's stomach with all his weight behind it. The stocky puncher grunted, but instead of backing away he drove in again with his head down. An uppercut that started somewhere near the ground slammed into the straw boss's face and he backed away.

Billy Joe could hear Whitey's breath whistling through his teeth. He was tiring badly. Billy Joe was certain of it. If he could stay on his feet for another minute, he'd have the fight won.

He wasn't expecting Whitey's next move. The straw boss reached behind him, to the thumb-thick iron rod that served to hold the coffeepot and the dutch oven over the flames of the campfire. He grabbed it and swung in one motion, and an instant later knew he'd made a mistake of considerable magnitude. The iron rod was hot, almost red-hot.

Billy Joe saw it, too. He stepped in under the upraised rod and locked both of his hands around Whitey's fist, the one that clutched the searing iron. The sizzle of scorching flesh was audible to every puncher in the circle of onlookers.

"Let go, damn you! Let go!"

Suddenly, Whitey didn't care if it sounded like he was begging. He was. The pain in the flesh of his hand was excruciating. Tears filled his eyes. His knees folded and he sank to the ground.

Billy Joe released his grip and the iron rod fell away. On his knees beside the fire, Whitey was bent forward in a posture of prayer. His burned hand was cradled in the other.

The drovers stood frozen, unprepared for so abrupt an end to the battle.

Chance looked around until his eyes found the cook.

"Get some grease. Pronto!"

Solomon hurried to the chuck box, procured a grease-coated can, and knelt beside the straw boss.

The cook opened the can and dipped into the grease, but a noise from the other man stopped him.

"Get the hell away," growled Whitey; then he plunged his blistered hand into the contents of the can.

Still on his knees, and with his right hand buried to the wrist in the can of grease, Whitey looked up into the face of Billy Joe.

"You're a dead man, Abilene. You just ain't realized it yet."

Chance nodded.

"Anytime you're ready."

Over behind the wagon, Arlo Smith caught up with Mule Hunnicutt, who was moving away quickly into the darkness.

"Seems like we had a little bet on that there fight," said Smith. "And your man lost."

Hunnicutt muttered an oath.

"It wasn't no fair fight. That new hombre, that Abilene. He cheated. You saw it."

In the darkness, Arlo Smith chuckled.

"He just outsmarted ol' Whitey, is what he done. He's pretty handy with his fists, too."

Mule Hunicutt swore again, this time with greater conviction.

"I could take him any day of the week in a fair, standup fight."

Smith was suddenly serious.

"I wouldn't sell that kid short, was I you, Mule. Looks like he's had some practice taking care of hisself."

Anger was growing in Hunnicutt. He and the straw boss went back a long way together. The newcomer had been lucky, that was all.

"Tell you what, old man," said Mule. "I'll bet you another twenty that Abilene fellow don't make it to Fort Sumner all in one piece. I just might be the man to see to it. Fists or six-shooters. Don't make me no difference."

"I'll take that bet, pardner," said Smith. "You just be sure you've made out your last will and testament 'fore you tangle with that young feller."

Mule Hunnicutt turned on his heel and stalked away, but Arlo Smith could hear him swearing even after he'd faded into the darkness.

Chapter Four

Gideon Stroop didn't allow the herd its usual grazing time before pointing the longhorns west. The sun was still somewhere below the eastern rim of the world when they moved out. The better part of a week lay between them and the Pecos River, and there wasn't a drop of water anywhere in that stretch of the Llano Estacado except what a man could wring from a prickly pear cactus.

Arlo Smith drifted in beside Billy Joe, riding the swing near the flank of the herd. For several minutes he occupied himself with worrying off a mouthful of Beach's Best. When he had the chaw firmly settled in his cheek and the plug stowed in a shirt pocket, he eyed Chance from beneath the soiled brim of his hat.

"Strikes me you have plenty of savvy when it comes to fightin'. Where'd you learn to use your fists like that?"

Chance looked the old man over for an interval of some duration, then grinned.

"I had an older brother who took it on himself to give me some instruction."

The old cowboy nodded.

"'Pears he done right well in the teachin'."

He paused before his next question. He knew he didn't have a right to ask, but he'd been around long enough to ignore some of the niceties of range etiquette. And besides, he sort of liked this long, lean cowboy who wasn't always bending a man's ear with worthless chatter.

"Where might that brother of yours be now?"

Chance was looking ahead, over the ears of his horse. His gaze didn't shift.

"Back in Tennessee."

"Tennessee, eh? Well, now. I had me some kinfolks

24

back in them Tennessee hills onct. Whereabouts might yours have been located?''

''The Cumberland country.''

''Is that so?'' Arlo Smith's idle curiosity was growing into something more. ''Mine was from farther west, over on the Duck River somewheres. Half of Texas must've come from that part of the South. Why, somebody said ol' Whitey hisself come from someplace in the Cumberland hill country.''

He waited, but Chance remained silent, so he continued.

''Your pa and ma and whole family still back there in them hills?''

''Yep.''

Arlo Smith sent a long stream of brown juice into a clump of bear grass.

''Didn't wanna come west, huh?''

Billy Joe didn't reply.

''Well,'' said Smith, ''some folks put down roots and just won't leave a place. Guess your family's sort of like that.''

''They're dead,'' said Billy Joe.

Arlo Smith looked sideways at Chance, then looked quickly away, to frown in annoyance at a little string of clouds that lay low on the horizon but weren't likely to get serious about anything. Then he wiped his mouth with the back of his hand.

''Hell, son. You'll have to forgive an old man for runnin' off at the mouth. I didn't mean to get plumb personal. Lots of folks back there lost their families to cholera and malaria and whatnot.''

Billy Joe had no desire to cause the garrulous old puncher embarrassment.

''Yeah. It was the cholera that took ma.''

A steer with one good horn and one that had grown in a loop to circle back and poke out his eye was drifting away from the main body of the herd. Smith kicked his horse into a lope and turned the stray back into the tide of cattle. Then he trotted back to Billy Joe's side.

''Oughta shoot that old steer so Solomon could make

some use of him," he said. "He'll wander off one of these days and get kilt by coyotes or butchered by Injuns."

Then, as though there had been no interruption, he said, "And a lot of families lost folks in the war. That's what happened to your pa, I guess."

Had it been anyone else, Billy Joe would have told him where to go. But there was no meanness in Arlo Smith's questions. The old man was hungry for talk.

"He got killed in a war, all right," said Chance. "But not the war you're talking about."

Smith waited, and fidgeted with his reins and scratched at his beard, and finally said:

"You don't have to tell me about it. I'll just shut my face and leave you be."

There was a half-grin on the young puncher's face. Arlo Smith remembered seeing it the night before, when the straw boss had stalked him beside the campfire, enjoying ambitious plans for cleaving the lean cowboy into several pieces, like a platter of Sunday fried chicken. But now, as then, there was no mirth in the grin.

"Well, it's been quite a spell. I was sixteen. There was a little fuss between pa and some folks who lived a couple of ridges over. Had to do with an old sow and a litter of pigs that belonged to pa. They got out of the pen and those other folks claimed 'em."

He stopped talking.

"Had yourselves some fight, I reckon," prompted Smith.

"Not much. When pa and I went to their place to get the pigs, the old man sicced his hound on us. Pa shot the dog and we took the pigs home."

Smith chuckled.

"Your pa sounds like pretty much of a man."

But he could tell the young man's thoughts were far away when he answered.

"Yeah. He was that."

The story was getting too good to turn loose of. Arlo Smith was figuring a way to get the young cowboy to go on with his narrative, but he ran out of time. A sudden cloud of dust boiled up behind them and the trail boss drew his horse to a walk.

"You fellers enjoyin' the outing?"

Smith shifted the cud of tobacco to his other cheek and turned a calm gaze on Stroop's face. It was clear to Billy Joe that Arlo Smith, for all his talkativeness, wasn't the kind to back down, not even from a testy trail boss.

"It ain't too bad. Except the beer ain't very cold," said Smith.

Stroop didn't see the humor in it. To Billy Joe he said:

"Abilene, go get yourself a fresh hoss. You're gonna take a little ride."

Billy Joe nodded. The trail boss waved a hand toward the west, where the sky and the earth met in an almost indiscernible line.

"Take a look in that direction for a couple of days. I wanna know what we're up against between here and the Pecos."

Then he fixed Billy Joe with a somber gaze.

"And maybe that'll give Whitey a chance to cool off. I don't want you two jaybirds shootin' holes in each other till we get where we're going."

The trail boss put the spurs to his mount and vanished in another whirlwind of dust.

"Sounds like you're hired on permanent," said Smith to Billy Joe.

"Yep. If those Comanches out there will let me draw my pay."

He reined about and loped away toward the remuda, now in the hands of Julio, the Mexican puncher who had escorted the freshly widowed old woman and the brittle corpse of her husband back to Fort Picket.

Arlo Smith watched Chance ride away and muttered to himself. Danged if it didn't look like he'd have a long wait before hearing the rest of that young cowpoke's history.

Chance chose his own dun horse for the ride into that strange, new, forbidding country. The trail that Stroop had sent him to follow was clear enough. First chiseled from the raw frontier by a gritty, stubborn old cowman named Charles Goodnight, it had been the avenue of successive cattle drives for several years now. But there were still no guarantees that a man could take a herd through to Fort Sumner, over in the raw, untamed territory called New Mexico, and live to tell his grandkids about it.

The Comanches, fiercest of the horse warriors, knew as certainly as a new season would come that their claim to the Staked Plains was nearing its end. Many had already seen the futility of resisting the dog soldiers and had accepted the inevitability of reservation confinement. But there were a few braves, no more than a handful, who would not be cowed into submission. If it meant their lives as forfeit, they would remain free and unfettered.

With some coffee and a fistful of jerky and a can of tomatoes in his saddlebags, and his bedroll tied on behind him, Billy Joe set out on a westerly course that took him past the point of the herd. And there was Whitey, with his scorched right hand bound up uselessly in a sleeve hacked from a dirty shirt and riding a horse his friend Mule Hunnicutt had had to saddle for him.

Chance passed within thirty feet of the straw boss but there was no exchange of words. Billy Joe rode on, feeling a prickle along his spine. He knew Whitey's eyes were fixed there, enjoying the picture of what a .45 caliber slug would do to a fresh, smart-aleck cowhand. He felt better when a low hogback cut him off from Whitey's line of sight.

It was coming on sundown and he was looking for a place to camp when he saw the sign. Unshod ponies, too many to estimate accurately, had crossed the trail he was following. Chance scanned the horizon at every point of the compass, but there was nothing to see except scattered clumps of bear grass and prickly pear cactus and, in the shallow washes cut by once-a-year rains, some patches of mesquite.

He dismounted and dropped to his knees. The tracks were not old. The ridges around each hoof impression were still sharp, not yet broken down and rounded off by the scouring wind, and the tiny desert insects had had little time to leave their zigzag trails in the finely ground dust.

There was no question in Billy Joe's mind about the origin of those hoofprints. Comanches had been riding those ponies. But were they bound for their camp after a hunting trip or were they simply ranging here and there across the Llano, like a pack of hungry coyotes?

Chance remounted and rode on, his .44-40 Winchester carbine now cradled across the saddle in front of him. Idly, he wondered if Mr. Gideon Stroop might not have foreseen the possibility of his encountering Comanches on this scouting ride; foreseen it and decided it would be a convenient means of solving his straw boss's problem with the new hand. Or, thought Billy Joe abruptly, it might have been Whitey himself who had suggested the reconnaissance.

He rode on, the idea still gnawing at his thoughts like a hungry pup with a slicked-off bone. Whitey would bear watching. All the way to Fort Sumner.

Right now, though, the Comanches were his most pressing problem. Night was coming on and the Llano held few coverts for a man interested in making himself scarce. It was past sundown when he found what he had hoped to find—a dry wash, with a deeply gouged cutbank. Not much in the way of protection, but it would put him and his horse off the bald ridges.

Billy Joe unsaddled, staked the dun nearby to graze, and settled in the lee of the cutbank. There would be no fire for coffee. Cold biscuits and beef jerky would have to suffice tonight. He settled in his blankets, listening to the dun gelding cropping at the buffalo grass, and let the recollection of that long ago agony in the Tennessee backwoods slide into his thoughts again.

He had paid two men for their part in it, exactly as he had promised his pa while he sat helplessly by and watched him die. Now he wanted to forget it, but the ledger still seemed out of balance. Would it always be that way? Would it eat on his conscience for the rest of his life?

Chance slept with the wariness of an outlaw steer hiding in a wait-a-bit thicket, but the hoofbeats were almost on him before he came fully to his senses. Daylight was only beginning to crowd against the thick, predawn darkness in the east when he heard the muffled rhythm of horses' hooves, many of them.

His first thought was of his own horse. If the dun whinnied, the world was very shortly going to be without the services of one Billy Joe Chance. He willed his eyes to pierce the semidarkness across the dozen paces to the patch of grass where the dun was picketed. What he saw made him catch his breath. Old Lonesome was very much aware of the cavalcade of Indian ponies moving along the ridge above the cutbank. His ears were cocked forward, watching their silhouettes sail across the graying sky.

Chance felt his scalp prickle, as though it were insecurely attached to his skull.

The dun horse didn't make a sound, though, and the trotting hoofbeats grew fainter and fainter. Billy Joe took a breath, his first in a full minute. He grinned at Lonesome, threw him a silent kiss, and in another heartbeat was frozen into immobility.

The hooves of yet another horse were drumming against the hollowness of the cutbank. The last Comanche in the party was lagging far behind the main band, perhaps favoring a pony with a tender hoof, or catching up after a brief constitutional.

This time Lonesome couldn't resist. He watched the lone Indian pony draw nearer, then grunted a greeting. It was barely audible, a rumble from the depths of his powerful chest, but it was enough for the sharp ears of the Comanche horseman.

Billy Joe knew what was going through the Indian's head. It was too dark to see much except the dun's outline, but the warrior was suddenly counting his good fortune. Here was a lone pony, caught in a thicket of mesquite, waiting for a brave with the eyes of an eagle and the ears of a red fox to gather him in.

Should he shout to his companions now fading into the distance? Or might he not simply surprise them by casually riding up with the new horse in tow? Ah, the sun of his ancestors was still asleep and his hunting day was already a success.

The cutbank was steep, too steep for his horse to negotiate, so the young Indian slid to the ground, wrapped the single strand of rawhide that served him as a bridle about the stump of a bear grass, and started over the ledge into the creekbed.

A shower of dirt preceded him. Billy Joe backed against the concave bank and watched the bare, brown feet slide into view, no more than six inches from his face. The knife in Chance's hand was poised, ready to open a throat and shut off any sound this rash young brave might wish to make.

But his thrust with the long-bladed knife was a heartbeat too soon. Instead of the soft throat of the Indian, the blade ground against his breastbone and slid away. Surprise and pain wrenched an un-Comanche-like howl from the young warrior's lips.

The next strike of Chance's skinning knife cut short the yelp, but Billy Joe knew the damage had been done. He stooped, caught a handful of the Indian's thickly greased hair, and made one more quick movement with his knife. Then he jerked up his saddle, threw it across the dun's back, and in less than the fragment of a moment it took the dust to settle he was racing down the creekbed, away from the still-quivering body of the young Comanche and the band of warriors his howl of pain had alerted.

Chapter Five

The wind in his face gave him hope. He had a head start on the band of Indians and so far he had managed to stay out of sight in the deep gash of dry riverbed. But almost at the instant the thought came to him the steep bank of the dry wash fell away and he was left on the bare crown of a rolling ridge, as exposed to view as the blade of new sun already showing above the horizon to the east.

A glance back over his shoulder showed him the contingent of braves. Two of them had pulled up beside the pony of the unfortunate one who had thought only to gain himself a dun horse but who had instead passed through the door of the great tepee of his fathers.

Billy Joe heard the wail from their throats as they made the discovery. And the warriors still on horseback were spurred to new heights of lust for the blood of this lone enemy.

The high-pitched shrieks of the oncoming Comanches told Billy Joe they were well mounted and their horses were fresh. They must have camped for the night not far from his own temporary shelter in the dry wash. It was clear, then. The only thing that lay between him and death were the flying hooves of his horse.

He rode toward the rising sun, lying low in the saddle and pouring out his heart into the ears of the long-legged dun. The stakes of this horserace were higher than a few dollars or a round of drinks. His own scalp would be the price if he lost.

Every puncher knew that a horse of pure color such as the lineback dun could outdistance the ponies of the Plains Indians, he reminded himself. The paint horses they rode were showy, and any warrior with an ounce of pride would choose a gaudily marked mount anytime he had a choice. But the whites and blacks and browns of the paints and pintos were nothing more than evidence of generations of inbreeding. Every puncher who had ever sat around a campfire and bragged about his favorite cowhorse knew that.

Billy Joe thought these thoughts and hoped it was more than just bragging.

Lonesome was running easily, his long legs eating up the distance in great strides. The thunder of hooves from the horses of his pursuers was not growing louder. But neither was it diminishing.

Then a shot sounded behind him. Some brave was hoping for a fortuitous hit, but the distance was too great and the back of a running horse made marksmanship a matter of luck.

Over his shoulder Chance saw them coming, not in a bunch now, but strung out. The slower horses were already beginning to falter, to fall back. At the lead of that pack of howling braves, though, was a horse of a different kind. It was a dark horse, a blood bay, its color made even more striking by the blood-red rays of the new sun.

And that horse was coming on!

A few shots would slow that charge and give him some breathing room, Billy Joe decided. He drew his six-gun, turned in his saddle, and fired at the lead figure. Against the shriek of the wind, the shots from his pistol sounded woefully feeble. The hammer fell on the last cartridge in the cylinder and still that brave drove ahead.

It became, then, a two-horse race. And within the single beat of a drumming hoof, a truth struck Billy Joe a staggering blow. The blood bay was a faster horse than his own. The Indian on the bay's back knew it. The yells from his throat were exultant now, as little by little the distance between the two horses shrank, like a strip of wet rawhide drawing up under a blazing sun.

A quick glance over his shoulder told Chance the Indian had a rifle. It was not a fancy-shooting carbine, but an old single-shot, on the order of a Remington rolling block, perhaps. The wild-eyed brave was close enough to use it, too, but he made no move to swing the muzzle toward his quarry, and Chance understood. This Comanche was a proud warrior, one who chose to fight his enemy at close quarters, close enough to read the fear of death in terror-stricken eyes, if such fear there was.

Billy Joe leaned low in his saddle. Under the maturing sun apprehension traced a cold finger down his spine. And it was at that instant he felt the first faltering in the stride of the dun horse. Lonesome was running on heart now, and heart would not be enough. The tattoo of hooves on the earth behind him told him all he needed to know. The Comanche brave was almost near enough to lean out and touch him.

It was clear that this Indian didn't intend to waste a bullet. Not when he could club this foolish white eyes from his saddle with the butt of his rifle.

The hot breath of eternity was singeing the hair on the neck of Billy Joe Chance. From the depths of that desperation an idea grew. And instantly he translated the thought into the deed. He clamped his knees against the dun's sides and sat back on the reins with a terrible suddenness.

The dun horse had done it a thousand times before. His forelegs shot forward in a stiff brace against the prairie sod. It was a maneuver any well-trained roping horse could execute instantly, with precision.

. It brought horse and rider to a sudden, jarring halt. The blood bay shot past them in a blur of red-black motion, the rifle in the hand of the Indian brave still upraised, ready to strike.

Billy Joe reached and drew his own Winchester from the boot at his knee. The Comanche had suddenly become the hunted instead of the hunter. He was trying frantically to get his horse turned around, his rifle brought to the ready.

Chance shot him through the rib cage, just under his armpit. The heavy slug jerked the Indian from the horse and sent him spinning to the ground, his limbs flopping limply like the legs of a freshly killed jackrabbit.

Freed of its rider, the bay horse slowed. Billy Joe spurred the dun beside it and caught up the loop of rawhide that served as a war bridle. With the Comanche's mount in tow, he pushed on in a run, but a quick backward glance told him the warriors' pursuit had ended. Two of their number had fallen. The price for the scalp of this paleskin, upon whom the gods of good fortune smiled, had become too high.

It was a day's ride and some to the east where the herd was moving at a snail's pace. Chance saw the lifting snake of dust climbing toward the sky long before he came in sight of the dark shadow of movement against the tan blanket of dry, curling buffalo grass that carpeted the Llano Estacado. By the time he came within sound of the bawling herd, the sun had vanished beyond the western horizon and Stroop and his drovers had settled the long-horns for the night.

Riding in toward the remuda, Billy Joe wondered idly

if the straw boss with the burned hand had improved in disposition since last they'd looked into each other's eyes. Whitey didn't seem the type to forgive quickly such minor trespasses committed against his person.

The nighthawks were at their posts around the herd and the main body of punchers had unsaddled, shaken the kinks out of their legs, and were lined up to fill their tin plates at the back of Solomon's chuck wagon. It was Julio now who was doing what Runt Maples had done, throwing up the temporary barricade around the remuda.

The young Mexican watched as Billy Joe rode up on the dun, the blood bay on the lead behind him. The bay was setting back against the lead, wild-eyed, his nostrils flaring. The odors of a white man's camp, perhaps once familiar, were now strange and frightening.

"Ah, Señor Abilene," said the Mexican wrangler. "Such a horse you have there. You have been away doing some horse trading, maybe?"

"You might say that, Julio," replied Chance. "I picked him up for little or nothing. Keep your eye on him, will you?"

"Of a certainty, amigo," said the Mexican.

When Billy Joe stepped into the light of the buffalo-chip fire, Stroop momentarily looked startled.

"When the hell did you get back?" the trail boss demanded. "I wasn't lookin' for you back for another day, anyway."

"I took a hankering for some of Solomon's grub, so I came on back early," said Billy Joe.

Whitey was sitting cross-legged on the ground not far away, with Mule Hunnicutt at his elbow. The scowl on Whitey's face answered the question Chance had asked himself earlier.

"Looks to me like we've got us a scout that'd rather do his scoutin' in camp," growled the straw boss.

"You run across anything of interest?" asked Stroop.

"Not much. No water. Just a few Indians," said Chance.

Stroop straightened suddenly.

"Comanches? Whereabouts?"

"A day's ride. About due west, I'd judge."

Stroop swore.

"I was hopin' we'd reach the Pecos without running into any redskins. They get sight of you?"

"Yep."

Whitey shoved a piece of sourdough bread into his mouth.

"They saw the tail end of his horse going over the ridge, I'd guess," he said.

"You close enough to get a count on 'em?" asked the trail boss.

"Half a hundred, I'd imagine," answered Billy Joe. "Hunting party, maybe."

"Hell," snorted Whitey around the mouthful. "Probably nothin' but a handful of squaws and old men. My guess is he was hightailin' it the other way too fast to tell if they were Indians or a bunch of antelope."

Billy Joe turned and fixed his gaze on the straw boss.

"I brought you a little something, Whitey. You can judge for yourself."

He reached into his shirt pocket, fished in it for a moment, and tossed what he found there toward the straw boss, sitting with his plate in his lap. The small, dark object flew through the smoke of the fire and landed with a splat in the beans on Whitey's plate.

Whitey looked down at the object that had landed in his meal. With his fork, held awkwardly in the hand that still wore the soiled bandage, he poked at the small, strange scrap of brown lying in the beans.

Abruptly, with the suddenness of a man who discovers that a red ant has journeyed well up his pants leg, the straw boss sprang to his feet. The fork, the tin plate, and the food in it flew from him.

"You son of a bitch!"

It was Arlo Smith, finished with his meal and hunkered on his heels with a cup of coffee, who reached out and picked up the object from the dust.

He wiped it off on his chaps, turned it over, and then over again, and began chuckling. The chuckle grew into a belly laugh.

"Well? What in tarnation is it?" another of the drovers demanded.

Arlo Smith paused long enough to catch his breath.

"An ear. A human ear, by damn," he said, and burst into laughter again.

He handed the bit of curling gristle to the drover squatted at his side. After giving it a close inspection, that man in turn passed it on. In minutes the ear of the young Comanche warrior had passed through the hands of every puncher gathered in the circle of firelight.

Billy Joe had kept his eyes on the straw boss. Whitey's bandaged hand was on the butt of the Colt at his hip but he knew it was a futile effort. It would be a time yet before he could grasp the butt of a gun with anything resembling his former skill.

In that instant, Mule Hunnicutt saw his opportunity. It was the time to put this fresh young jackass in his place and ensure his continued niche within the good graces of the straw boss. On his feet and two paces away from where Whitey stood, Mule went for his six-gun.

It was almost comical to Billy Joe Chance. He let the big man's hand start its descent. When the big, square-tipped fingers started to curl about the walnut grips, Chance drew. In the flickering yellow light of the camp-fire, the movement was barely discernible. The other drovers knew he had drawn because the gun was there in his hand. But, like the whip of a hummingbird's wing, there hadn't been much to see.

Mule Hunnicutt stood with the barrel of his own gun still in leather and looked into the muzzle of the .45 caliber Colt in the hand of the man called Abilene. He swallowed at nothing in particular and let the gun find its own way back into his holster.

Gideon Stroop was angry.

"Put that hogleg away!" he barked at Billy Joe. "I told you I wouldn't put up with any gunplay when there's a chance of spookin' this herd."

Billy Joe shrugged.

"His choice," he said.

And he slid the weapon back into its holster.

The blood bay horse of the Comanche brave who was now residing in the Great Lodge with the spirits of the war chiefs was off to himself in the rope corral when Billy Joe went to saddle up the following morning. There was no doubt that the bay had at some point in the past belonged to a white man. There was even a brand low on his left shoulder, a simple jagged line that resembled a bolt of lightning.

But it had been a long time since this horse had worn the cumbersome saddle of a Texas cowboy. Arlo Smith and Julio and three or four other drovers watched as Billy Joe roped him out of the remuda.

"You got yourself a handful, young feller," observed Arlo Smith. "I do declare I'd just as leave screw my saddle onto the back of a catamount."

Chance took off his shirt.

"Well, do me a favor and hang on to this rope while I put a blindfold on this catamount," he said.

While Arlo Smith anchored the lead rope, Chance wrapped his shirt around the bay's eyes. Then, standing clear of the hooves, Billy Joe swung his saddle onto the horse's back. There was no movement from the bay. He stood spraddle-legged and trembling, but immobile.

The other drovers, aware of the drama that was fixing to make this routine morning chore a bit special, were fiddling with ropes or giving their own cinches a second inspection. They wanted to be around when this cowboy who was so handy with his fists and his gun got himself a handful of mean-tempered bronc.

Saddled and bridled, the horse Arlo Smith had compared to a catamount had still made no move to fight. Standing close to his shoulder, Billy Joe slipped a foot into the stirrup, swung aboard with a minimum of time and motion, and nodded to Smith.

The older cowboy jerked away the blindfold.

For a full quarter-minute, the blood bay made no move. He rolled his eyes, taking in the remuda, the herd of longhorns swelling into movement, the unfamiliar wagon nearby, and the semicircle of watching drovers.

Then he dropped the hammer.

He sprang straight upward, swapped ends in a movement not unlike that of a big cat, and came to earth with a stiff-legged jolt that snapped Billy Joe's chin against his chest. Then the bay erupted in a series of chain-lightning explosions. One second he was turning his belly to the dawning sky, the next he was standing on his head with his hindquarters switching like the tail of a surprised rattlesnake.

Once he flipped over, landing on his back against the hard, dry earth. Billy Joe saw it coming, stepped out of the saddle, and was back astride it before the bay had again gained his feet.

Caught up in the excitement, the other punchers were whooping and waving their hats, urging the rider on. They knew masterful bronc-busting when they saw it.

Arlo Smith had waved the shirt in the face of the jittery bay to help him make up his mind, and now he stood to one side, grinning broadly, while his friend Abilene put a fair-to-middlin' ride on this fine piece of horseflesh. Then he saw Mule Hunnicutt astride his own horse a few feet away.

Arlo Smith couldn't resist.

"Hey, Mule," he called. "I'll give you a chance to get some of your money back. I'll bet you another twenty he stays with that old pony."

But the sting of his first loss still burned painfully in the breast of Mule Hunnicutt.

"Aw, you go to hell," he growled.

It was a long time before the bay began to wear down, and Billy Joe had a painful moment of uncertainty. But then he sensed the change. The Comanche pony's moves were not as razor-edged, and his leaps no longer carried him up where the air was thin.

But the man in the saddle didn't want there to be any question left in this bronc's head about who was boss. He raked the horse from shoulder to flank with his spurs.

The blood bay had had all he wanted. His bucking turned into a series of halfhearted crowhops and then he trotted in a little circle before yielding to the pressure of the unfamiliar bit in his jaws.

Not a word passed among the punchers who had

watched the performance, but here and there Billy Joe detected a nod and a grin. It was about all the praise a man would likely get.

Gideon Stroop had been among those witnessing the ride. Now he jerked a thumb toward the herd.

"You boys think this is the Fourth of July? We've got three thousand longhorns that're dry as a shuck, and two days of drivin' before we get a look at the Pecos. Let's get 'em to movin'."

The mood of the longhorns had undergone a subtle change. On this day, all they wanted was to bawl and mill about and hook at anything that came within reach. Finally, reluctantly, they strung out in a ragged westward line.

Arlo Smith rode up beside Billy Joe and gingerly passed the shirt to him.

"Don't worry about old Catamount here," Chance reassured him. "He's gonna behave himself. He's through playing Comanche."

Smith worried off a chew of tobacco and returned the plug to his pocket.

"One of these days I'd like to hear how you come by that there dandy bay hoss," he said. "If a man was to believe Julio, he'd suppose you got him in a horse trade."

"You might say that," replied Chance. "Me and that Comanche brave had us a long, serious parley about this horse. I finally had to give him some boot."

Arlo's grunt was sarcastic.

"Yeah. I'll bet you did."

The conversation ended abruptly. The longhorns were growing rebellious. Here and there one would take a sudden notion to leave the herd and head over the nearest ridge. Or lower his head and charge a horse and rider that moved in too close. Their craving for water had dulled their senses, like a dog gone mad with hydrophobia.

It was not until midafternoon that Arlo Smith found himself riding again beside the young puncher on the blood bay horse.

"We'll have us some fun keepin' this bunch of loco steers together by tomorrow," he said. But it was clear to

Billy Joe that the older cowboy had more on his mind than talk about thirsty longhorns. He waited.

Finally, Arlo Smith said, "T'other day you were telling me about your family back in the hills of Tennessee. And something about a squabble with another bunch of hill folks."

"That's right."

"Well," Smith said, the word turning up on the end in the form of a question, but then he paused. He turned his head and ejected a stream of brown juice and wiped his mouth on his shirtsleeve. "Them Tennessee kinfolks of mine I mentioned? They used to tell a yarn about a feud back in the Cumberland hills. On one side was a pack of shiftless folks name of O'Bannon, I believe."

He scowled at the twitching ears of his horse.

"Cain't properly recollect the name of them other folks. But it was one dandy fuss, I hear tell."

He shot a glance at Billy Joe from the corner of his eye. The face of the younger man was devoid of expression.

"Well, never mind. The name'll come to me. It allus does, sooner or later."

Billy Joe's gaze was on the far distant horizon, where the lead steer was topping a windswept ridge before sinking from sight. It was a long time before he spoke, and Arlo Smith had decided he had reached a dead end.

"Chance," said Billy Joe.

"What?"

"The name you're looking for. Chance."

Arlo Smith snapped his fingers, causing the blood bay to jerk his head up.

"Yeah. That's it. That's the name of the other bunch."

He nodded his head vigorously.

"The Chance-O'Bannon feud. Yessirree bob. That was it, all right."

The graying puncher cocked his head at his companion and squinted through one eye.

"S'funny you'd recollect that name right off like that. Less'n you know more about the feud than I do."

Billy Joe was still looking into the distance.

"I know about it," he said.

They rode on in silence for some minutes. Finally, Arlo Smith spoke again.

"You know somethin'? You ain't never mentioned your name, young feller."

"That's a fact," Chance grunted.

Arlo Smith was at the point of exasperation. He had dangled all sorts of bait in front of this closemouthed fish and his quarry wouldn't take the hook. He decided to confront the problem head-on.

"Your name wouldn't happen to be the same as the folks on one side of that fight, would it?"

It was a time of hard decision for Billy Joe Chance. He'd kept the bitter memories locked up tight inside him, and he'd been careful not to advertise his name to the world. But maybe it was time.

"I'll tell you a little tale, Mr. Arlo Smith," he said. "If you think you can keep your mouth shut."

Arlo Smith's eyes gleamed.

"You bet I can. Silent as a graveyard. That's me."

Billy Joe cocked an eyebrow.

"Yeah, I can tell you ain't much of one for talking."

A cloud momentarily darkened Arlo Smith's countenance.

"Well, we're talkin' between friends, now. Friends has got some rights, you know."

Billy Joe waved the comment aside.

"I'll tell you about that feud between the Chances and the O'Bannons if you're dead set on hearing it. And if you can keep it to yourself."

Arlo Smith licked his lips.

"Damn," said Billy Joe. "There goes that old crooked-horned steer again. Better chouse him back . . ."

"Oh no you don't," bawled Smith. "I'll get that steer back in line. I want you right here, oiled up and ready to spin that yarn when I get back."

And he gigged his pony toward the one-eyed long-horn that insisted on leaving the herd and drifting toward the Rio Grande or whatever else the world had to offer in that direction.

In less than a minute he was back.

"You were sayin' . . . ?"

Chapter Six

"**A**fter the cholera took ma, there was just the three of us, pa and Tom Roy and me. I was fifteen goin' on sixteen. Tom Roy was a couple of years older."

The young man's voice was even, without emotion. He could have been talking about the weather.

"We had a little bottomland, enough to raise some pigs and some chickens and a little corn and such. Pa was figuring on clearing another forty acres. Then he had the run-in with the O'Bannons."

"Your pa's name. What was it?" Arlo Smith interrupted.

"Ruben. Ruben Chance," said Billy Joe, and the older cowboy nodded to himself. Uh-huh. That was the name they'd talked about.

But the narrative had stopped, and Arlo Smith wished he hadn't interrupted. It took a heap of patience to get this young rooster to string together more than a dozen words at one time.

Finally Smith grunted.

"You told me about the O'Bannons layin' claim to a sow and a litter of pigs that rightfully belonged to your pa. What happened after you and him went to get 'em?"

Billy Joe nodded.

"Like I said, old man O'Bannon sicced his dog on us. Pa just shot the dog and we took the sow and the pigs and went home. That's all there was to it."

He frowned, the memories coming back.

"We thought it would end right there. But a week later, a little more, maybe, we came in from clearing timber one day. That old sow and all her pigs were dead. They'd taken an ax to 'em. And for good measure they'd killed our boar, too."

"So what'd your pa do?"

"Went looking for the O'Bannons. He told Tom Roy and me to stay home, but we followed him. He found two of the O'Bannons cutting wood. Tom Roy and I hid in the underbrush and watched.

"Pa wasn't one for wasting a lot of time on talk. He just walked up and coldcocked one of those fellows with his fist, and when the other one came at him with a hand ax, he took it away from him and broke his arm.''

Arlo Smith glanced sideways at the young puncher on the glistening bay horse. That slight grin was there again, but now he knew it didn't mean there was humor in the thoughts of this man named Chance.

It reminded him.

"You never did tell me your front name," said Arlo Smith.

"It don't much matter," said his companion. "I'm the only one left.''

Arlo Smith gritted his teeth until his jaws ached. He'd wait the kid out if it took the rest of the day, what there was left of it.

Chance didn't seem to be paying much attention to his apt listener, however. He rode on, his eyes touching the herd and then flickering out to run along the horizon.

He was still looking into the distance when he spoke again.

"There was a whole passel of those O'Bannons. They rode over not long after that and shot up our place. No one got hurt, to speak of. Except one of them. He tried to sneak up and set fire to the cabin where pa and Tom Roy and I were holed up. Tom Roy put one in his leg. But it didn't kill him.''

Billy Joe hooked a knee over his saddlehorn and rolled a Bull Durham cigarette. It took so long that Arlo Smith was starting to mutter under his breath.

"It was while the whole bunch of them was laid up around the cabin taking potshots at us that old man O'Bannon just up and died. A heart attack, we figured, but the O'Bannons blamed it on us just the same.''

"Yeah, it figgers," said Arlo Smith, careful that his

words didn't get in the way of whatever else this survivor
of the Chance-O'Bannon feud might have to say.

"It was quiet for a time after that. They buried their
dead and backed off. Finally it looked safe, so one day pa
took the wagon and headed for the settlement to get some
cartridges and things. I went with him. We left Tom Roy
there to watch after the place."

"It was a bad mistake."

Abruptly, he broke off. Arlo Smith, engrossed in the
tale, was aware with only half a mind of the stream of
longhorn cattle moving beside them. When Chance spurred
the red-black horse into a sudden run, he saw what was
happening. At the head of the column, the tide of steers
had split around a spire of stone that jutted out from the
crest of a little rise. With inexplicable, thirst-dulled senses,
one tongue of the phalanx of cattle simply swung about
and boiled down a broad, deep ravine, like a torrent of
water released into a streambed.

The dozen and a half punchers rode hard but the sun
was long down and only a thin wisp of daylight showed by
the time they had bunched the herd again. Stroop, silhouetted against the gun-barrel blue of the sky, waved his hat
over his head, the signal to settle 'em in for the night.

Arlo Smith rode toward Billy Joe in the failing light,
and they both saw the straw boss, Whitey, coming at a
lope.

"You two get yourselves a pair of fresh hosses. You'll
be wet-nursin' these critters for a spell," said Whitey.

Billy Joe pulled up. Whitey looked at him, the cutting
edge of his voice clear in the stillness.

"What's the matter, Abilene? Was you figurin' on
doin' a little sleepin' tonight?"

Billy Joe ignored the sarcasm in the comment.

"Tell you what we ought to do. We're not much more
than a day's drive from the Pecos River right now. We'd be
better off keeping these longhorns on the move right on
through the night. We could make the river by the middle
of the morning."

Whitey snorted.

"Hell! Whoever heard of pushing a bunch of outlaw steers at night?"

Billy Joe's voice was steady.

"Buck Pauley did it on the Abilene trail. And I heard that old man Goodnight drove through a couple of nights on this trail right here."

There was venom in Whitey's words.

"If you're so damned smart, why ain't you bossin' the outfit? Just go get those horses like you was told to."

Arlo Smith grunted a four-letter word.

"You don't mind if we get us a bite to eat afore we start some more wear and tear on our hip pockets from these saddles?"

"You can worry about fillin' yore bellies with frijoles after we get to the Pecos. Savvy?"

He jerked his mount around, sank his spurs deep into the sorrel's sides, and was gone in a cloud of alkali dust that hung suspended in the dusky stillness for a long time.

"Nice feller," said Chance.

"Yeah. Reminds me of a porcupine. There ain't no way to get on his good side 'cause he don't have one."

They rode to the remuda in the failing light, roped out fresh horses, and shifted their saddles.

Billy Joe started away, riding back toward the herd, but Arlo Smith reined up.

"You go on," he said. "I'll catch up in a minute."

It was some time before the old cowboy came drifting up through the uncertain light shed by the prairie stars. Billy Joe and a half-dozen other drovers were easing around the periphery of the herd. On the far side, a gravel-voiced cowboy was singing a song about ridin' ol' Paint and leadin' ol' Dan.

It was too dark to see the man who rode up but Billy Joe recognized the dapple gray of the horse he was riding.

"Long minute," he said.

The silence went on for some little time.

"Hell, I was just fetchin' us a couple pieces of pone."

It was Arlo Smith's voice but there was something wrong with it.

"Sounds like you've got a mouthful of mush," Chance said. "What happened?"

"Aw, that damned Whitey," said Arlo Smith. "He rode up just as I was fixin' to leave the chuck wagon."

"What'd he do?"

"He threw a wall-eyed fit. Then he took a poke at me."

Billy Joe pulled up.

"How bad?"

"Nothin' much. Split my lip open. And I think the son of a gun chipped a tooth. I don't have many of them to spare, either."

Billy Joe studied about it for a while.

"I guess he's taking it out on you because you and me have got friendly," he said. "I'll have another little talk with him."

"You'll by damn do no such thing," growled Arlo Smith. "When the day comes that I gotta have somebody else fight my fights is when I hang it up."

Chance shrugged.

"Up to you."

A few million stars floated low over the Llano Estacado, giving off enough light to show Billy Joe the outline of the herd, and when other riders drifted out from time to time to relieve the early nighthawks. But no one came to relieve him or Arlo Smith.

They met again on the far side of the circle. Smith's humor hadn't improved. He tested his swollen lip with his fingers.

"If it wouldn't set these crazy longhorns to runnin', I'd go have it out with that straw boss right now. I used to be pretty handy with a six-gun."

Billy Joe grinned in the darkness.

"I'll try to hold 'em if you wanna go call him out and see who's got the fastest trigger finger." He paused. "Where would you like the remains sent?"

"Thanks a heap," growled Smith. "You shore fill a man full of confidence."

He fished the plug of tobacco from his shirt pocket,

bit off a chew, and swore again as the tobacco burned his lacerated lip.

"Now, if I could handle a six-shooter like you can, Chance, I'd be struttin' around like a banty rooster, darin' any *hombre* to look at me cross-eyed." He wiped his mouth carefully with a sleeve. "Where'd you get so handy with a hogleg?"

Billy Joe saw it coming. It was Arlo Smith's not very subtle way of opening up the subject he'd been pursuing for a week.

He didn't feel like making it easy.

"What're you doin', Smith? Writing a shoot-'em-up windy for one of those big Eastern newspapers? You sure have a fair share of curiosity."

"I might be. I just might be, you young smart aleck," snorted Arlo Smith. "Anyway, I might if I knowed how to write anything more'n my name."

Billy Joe had known he'd have to tell the rest of it, once he got started. If not to Arlo Smith, then to someone else. It had been eating at him for nearly six years now, consuming him slowly, inch by inch, like a bull snake swallowing a chicken that was too big for his gullet.

"The learnin' of a six-gun came later.

"Like I was telling you, pa and me set out for town in the wagon. We were low on grub and low on shells after that little set-to with the O'Bannons. Tom Roy was to stay at the house.

"Looking back on it, it seems like a pretty dumb thing to do. But we figured the O'Bannon bunch would lay low for a while. Especially since the old man had died."

Arlo Smith couldn't see it, but he knew Chance was rolling himself a cigarette by feel in the darkness. He waited until the younger man fired a match on the butt of his rifle and, concealing the glow in his cupped hands, touched it to the tobacco.

"Looks to me like you folks would have been hightailing it to find the sheriff," said Smith.

A chuckle, grimly humorless, sounded from the throat of the younger cowboy.

"The sheriff was a shirttail cousin to the O'Bannons.

Hell, everybody in that part of Tennessee was kin to 'em, one way or another.

"It had been raining some and pa's mules were having a tough time of it on that old mountain road. We were in a thick stand of timber when a dozen of 'em came at us on horseback. Pa would have shot it out with the bastards. I know he would. But he was afraid I'd catch a slug."

"Who was in the bunch?" asked Arlo Smith.

"The two boys that pa had whipped were leading it. Two of the brothers, Newt and Calvin. I never did get a good look at the others. They rode off through the trees while we were looking down the barrels of those two boys' rifles."

The silence drew out, long and painfully.

Then Billy Joe went on.

"They made pa drive the wagon up a canyon, to an old place that somebody had moved off and left. There was a barn still standing. It was about all there was."

He took a long drag on the cigarette, curled his leg around his saddlehorn, and stubbed out the butt against his bootheel. In the hot, still air that lay over the bedded herd, Arlo Smith felt a sudden chill. He didn't think he was going to particularly enjoy the rest of this tale.

"Well, we went inside the barn. There was some moldy hay and a couple of milking stalls and a bunch of pigeons. Nothing else to speak of. Except a three-legged milking stool.

"Pa had an idea what was going to happen. I could see it in his face. They had his hands tied behind him. I made a run at the littler one, Calvin, and managed to kick him between the legs, but all I got for my troubles was a sock on the head with the butt of his rifle."

Chance slid his hat to the back of his head. In the scattering of light from the stars Arlo Smith saw his features. They were hard and bitter, as though chiseled from a wedge of granite by an angry sculptor.

"I was out for a spell. When I came to, they had me

tied to one of those milking stalls. And those O'Bannons knew how to tie a man, I can tell you."

Arlo Smith cleared his throat.

"Where was your pa?"

"It took me a while to get my eyes in focus. Then I saw him. They'd tied his hands and his feet and had a rope around his neck."

"You mean he was still alive?"

"Yeah. The O'Bannon boys had stood him on the milking stool, put the loop around his neck, and tied the rope to a rafter. It was pretty tight, but not tight enough to choke him.

"He was all right as long as he stood straight. And didn't kick the milking stool over."

Arlo Smith was wondering why he had ever insisted on hearing the story of the Chance-O'Bannon feud. It was no longer just another entertaining yarn.

"Well, I guess . . ." he said, and let the sentence trail off for want of something intelligent to say.

Chance went on as though he hadn't heard the words.

"That was the middle of the morning. I tried my damnedest to get loose but they'd tied me with wire. There wasn't any way.

"Pa managed to bear it until almost dark. He was some man, was pa. He said to me, 'Billy Joe, you do what you have to do about those O'Bannons. But there's some good in life, too. Don't you go throwing that away.' "

He stopped. Even the stars had moved before he spoke again.

"Along about sundown pa got too tired to stand it. And then the milking stool turned over."

Arlo Smith looked away, at the outline of the herd of longhorns, and then eastward, where a thumbnail sliver of moon was sliding into view. He had forgotten about the pain in his swollen lip.

"I got loose a long time later. Took pa down and put him in the wagon and drove on home."

"Your brother . . . ?" Arlo Smith left the sentence dangling.

"I'm just glad pa never knew what the rest of that bunch did to Tom Roy."

Finally, Arlo Smith asked, "What did you do?"

"Well, I buried pa and Tom Roy under a tree up on the hill and went looking for the O'Bannons."

"Find 'em?"

"Yep."

"Filled 'em full of lead, I'd reckon," said Arlo Smith with satisfaction.

"Nope." In the half-light, Billy Joe grunted. Arlo Smith wasn't certain if it was meant to be an expression of humor, so he kept quiet.

"I had pa's old navy Colt. I finally located Newt at the sawmill down the river. I was gonna be fair. That's the way pa would have wanted it. I called him out and even got off a shot. But, hell. I wasn't any match for him. I managed to crawl away in the bushes and hide. Nearly bled to death before I got back to the place."

"Then you come west, I guess," said Smith.

"Not right then. I sold off everything I could and bought me a new gun and a wagonload of cartridges and went back up in the hills. I lived with that Colt every day, from daylight till dark. After four months I damn well knew which end of the barrel the bullet came out of."

Chance chuckled and this time Arlo Smith knew that the thought in Billy Joe's mind was giving him pleasure.

"The O'Bannons, Newt and Calvin, were in town when I found them. They thought I was still a wet-eared kid and they were going to swallow me in one bite. But when the lead stopped flyin' they were just sort of laying around waitin' for the undertaker.

"That's when I figured I'd better head west."

Arlo Smith allowed himself a laugh.

"Have you ever run across any more of the O'Bannon bunch?"

In the moonlight, Smith could see that Chance's face had lost some of its bitterness.

"Nope. Haven't seen hide nor hair of 'em. And I reckon that's all right, too. Every now and then I remember what pa said: 'Don't go throwing away the good in life.'"

Suddenly, Billy Joe grinned at Arlo Smith.

"Old-timer, you know more about me than my own ma. But I'd just as soon you keep it to yourself."

"You can count on that, Billy Joe," replied Smith.

Chapter Seven

It was the young Mexican wrangler named Julio who first saw the Comanches in the burning sunlight of the following day. Every other puncher had his hands full trying to keep three thousand head of thirst-maddened longhorns from breaking into a run in an equal number of directions.

The Mexican abandoned the remuda he was charged with tending and spurred his mount in a dead run toward the lead steers, where an anxious Gideon Stroop was overseeing the chaos that a few days earlier had been a well-mannered trail herd. But Julio's shout was sufficiently loud that it carried from the point to the drag. And his outstretched arm and pointing finger answered the rest of the question.

"Señor Stroop!" he bellowed. "The Comanches. They are there. *Cientos!* Hundreds of them!"

The bald plateau of prairie concealed very little and it didn't hide the Indians. Billy Joe saw them, tiny specks on the horizon. Julio's shout had made it sound as though the redskins were hardly more than the span of a six-gun shot away.

The Mexican's estimate of numbers was somewhat less than precise, too. Chance watched the moving specks for a minute and grunted to himself. About half a hundred, the same number that had chased him. It was not out of reason to suppose that this was the same hunting party.

The only trouble with that was, Comanches had no difficulty making the transformation from hunting party to war party. And these Indians, if indeed they were the same, would not have forgotten that it was a Texan cowboy who had killed two of their number.

Billy Joe left his position at the flank of the herd and loped to the point, where Julio was at that moment telling Gideon Stroop in rapid-fire Spanish about the Indians: where, how many, and how unhappy would be his poor *madre* if her youngest son was rendered *muerto* by the bullet of a Comanche warrior.

"Shut up, Julio," Gideon Stroop said. "I ain't blind. I can see them Injuns. You get back there and mind those hosses. We sure will have trouble if they scatter and the Comanches take after 'em."

Stroop turned to Chance, just reining up the blood bay gelding.

"What do you say? Is that the same bunch that tried to get your scalp?"

Watching the movement of the tiny figures on the horizon, like so many distant antelope, Billy Joe nodded.

"I'd say so. About the same number."

"What do you suppose they have in mind?"

"Why, nothing much. Stealin' the herd. And the horses. Comanches can't resist horses."

"Oh, is that all?" Stroop grunted with sarcasm.

"Not exactly," said Billy Joe. "I'd say they figure on taking some paleface hair in exchange for the two braves I killed."

Stroop began to swear, and kept it up for a minute or more. Then he said, "Great. Just great. That's just what we needed. Less than a day from the Pecos and we've got the damned Injuns to worry about. If they run at us, this bunch of loco longhorns will scatter from hell to breakfast."

He broke off and watched the line of dark, slow-moving objects on the horizon.

"I had a feelin' about this drive from the day we started."

They both turned at the sound of approaching hoof-beats. It was the straw boss, Whitey.

"Them your amigos, Abilene? The ones you made friends with by killin' off a couple of 'em?"

Chance looked steadily at the straw boss.

"I'd say so." He grinned a humorless grin. "They say those Comanches have a real special hankering for white hair, too."

"You go to hell," Whitey snapped.

Stroop cut in.

"Nothin' to do except keep on drivin' the herd and hope we can stand 'em off. They've got us outnumbered three to one."

Billy Joe was watching the lead steer, the old fish-belly longhorn that had been the troublemaker. There was something about him that had a different look. He no longer had the appearance of an animal that was going to drop in his tracks any minute. His step was quicker. His head was up. Something had given him a new interest in life.

"We'd best get ready," Gideon Stroop was saying. "Those devils'll be comin' at us in another hour."

Billy Joe studied the lay of the land to the west. It was breaking up some now, the rolling prairie giving way to ragged hills and rock-studded canyons. The Llano Estacado was coming to an end as they drew nearer the bending, hooking course of the Pecos.

Directly ahead of the herd was a V in the rim of the hills that paralleled the broad valley of the river. It was through that notch the herd would have to move.

Stroop saw it too.

"That's where they'll hit us, boys. When we start through that gap yonder. Mark my words. They'll run in and cut up this herd any way they please. And us along with it."

The old fish-belly steer was past them now and stepping out quickly. Billy Joe saw him raise his head and swing his nose in a circle, testing the breeze from the west.

"You're right," he said to Stroop. "Those Comanches are headin' for that notch. But maybe we can give 'em a little surprise."

Stroop swung around.

"How's that?"

"Maybe it'll work, maybe it won't," said Chance.

"But keep the herd pointed toward that gap and we'll find out."

He gigged the bay horse forward.

"Right now I'm going to give 'em a little bait."

With the catamount bay in a run beneath him, Billy Joe stood in the stirrups and watched the single line of Comanche warriors drawing nearer. They hadn't seen him yet but it wouldn't be long.

The opening in the rim of jagged bluffs was simply a stone-formed funnel that gave onto the lower level of the river plain. Where the trail crested and started down, Chance pulled up and looked westward. Dimly, on the horizon, he could see a dark green line. That, he knew, had to be the Pecos River.

For his plan to work, the longhorns had to know it was there. He wet a finger and held it up. The slight breeze was still holding, coming at him from the west.

He swung his gaze to the right. Below him, on the flat bench of prairie that abutted the bluffs, he saw the Indians, strung out in single file and riding at a trot.

At the same instant, they saw him. The distance was too far for Billy Joe to hear the yells, but he didn't have to. The brave at the head of the column thrust his arm into the air and waved his rifle above his head. Suddenly, the line of Comanches was in a full run, directly at him.

It was not just the sight of a Texas drover that fired their thirst for blood. Chance understood that. It was the sight of the blood bay horse that really caused them to explode into rage. They wanted the scalp of this cowboy. They owed it to the ones of their number who had died by his hand.

Billy Joe turned and looked behind him. The herd had reached the mouth of the gap and was flowing into the throat of the defile.

But the mood of the longhorns had changed. The cattle were no longer moving at a shuffling, listless walk. Their pace had sharpened. Their heads were up, their huge horns swinging from side to side with the quickness of their stride.

The Pecos River was still five miles away but, after

ninety miles of bone-dry driving, the prairie breeze was carrying to their quickened senses the delectable scent of water!

As he watched, the mottled ranks of longhorns came suddenly alive. It was the same as it had been on the night that Runt Maples had been trampled into the earth. Led by the fish-belly steer, the cattle bounded forward. Their tongues hanging long and swollen from their mouths, they were instantly in a desperate run, racing toward the life-saving ambrosia carried to them on the late morning breeze.

Billy Joe saw the longhorns burst into a stampede and then he swung back around to check the progress of the four dozen Comanche warriors. They were close upon him, much closer than he had expected them to be. It was going to be close.

The yells of the Indians were loud in his ears now, as they drove their ponies up the slope toward the neck of the V in the line of rocky bluffs. A rifle shot sounded from the pack, and then another. Chance heard the bullets whine past him.

The fuse had been lit, the elements set into motion. It was time for him to back off and let the gods of fortune, or misfortune, take over.

He spurred the bay horse toward the point of the oncoming juggernaut of crazed cattle and, with inches to spare, squeezed through the channel between the tide of longhorns and the bulwark of boulders that formed the sides of the gap.

Then the running cattle were into the neck of the funnel and fanning out down the slope like the spearpoint of a millrace spewed suddenly forth by a ruptured dam.

The Indians, riding east, and the longhorns, stampeding to the west, met just where the slope broke sharply downward. Billy Joe heard the bloodcurdling battle cries of the warriors change abruptly to surprise, and then he heard nothing but the thunder of twelve thousand longhorn hooves spilling through the gap and down toward the plain below.

There was no way to see what was happening. He

didn't dare risk riding into the thirst-crazed herd. All he could do—and it was what the other drovers were doing—was to sit his horse and wait until the last of the plunging longhorns were through the throat of the stone divide.

The charging cattle passed. Chance, followed closely by Gideon Stroop and Whitey, rode through the notch of the bluffs.

Three of the Comanches had failed to escape the charge of longhorns. All three, and their horses with them, were on the ground at the top of the slope, beaten into the red bank of soil until man, horse, and earth were hardly distinguishable.

The other braves had vanished. In escaping the crush of stampeding cattle, they apparently had scattered in all directions. It would be a time before they were regrouped and eager to contemplate another attack on this particular herd of Texas longhorns and drovers. Such was Billy Joe's thought.

From the height of the bluffs, he and the others could watch the herd in its mad flight toward the Pecos. Red dust boiled upward, almost hiding the three thousand cattle beneath it. They would run until they reached water, or until they fell dead in their tracks.

"You had that figured down to a gnat's whisker, Abilene," said Gideon Stroop.

"A shade closer than I had in mind," replied Billy Joe.

Whitey reined his horse up and spat into the dirt beside the body of a Comanche warrior.

"You ain't gonna try to tell us you had this whole thing figured out? That them Injuns would get in the way of a stampede?"

Billy Joe pushed back his hat and eyed the straw boss.

"A snot-nosed kid could've put it together, Whitey. Why, with a week to study about it, you might even have done it yourself."

"You're gonna mouth off once too often. . . ."

Whitey's rejoinder was cut short by Stroop.

"Cut the jawin' and let's get to ridin'. We've got a

herd of cattle that are gonna take themselves a swim and we'd better be there when they do.''

The cattle had a lead but the punchers rode at a run. Then they began to see, here and there along the herd's path, steers that had used up the last of their strength. And when one had faltered, the crazed herd had swept on over him, beating him into the ground. For the few stragglers still alive, the trail boss motioned to a puncher behind him, instructing him to put them out of their misery with a .45 slug.

Chance, Whitey, and the trail boss caught up with the herd before it reached the banks of the Pecos.

"Try to slow 'em down," yelled Stroop.

But there was no slowing the longhorns. Might as well have tried to check a cyclone, Billy Joe grunted to himself.

Suddenly they were through the scrub cedars and into the swirling, sand-colored waters of the river, still swollen by the spring runoff from the mountains that gave birth to its headwaters. The steers in the lead wanted to stop and drink, but those coming behind pushed them on, and on, ever deeper into the river.

In minutes the broad ribbon of the Pecos was filled with longhorns, struggling to keep their noses out of the water. Then, what every puncher feared might happen, did. In the middle of the river, the longhorns began to mill, the point of the herd turning back upon itself like a snake coiling into its own length.

Billy Joe could hear Gideon Stroop's shout above the din of the bellowing, fear-crazed cattle.

"Keep 'em headed across. Don't let 'em mill!"

But it was too late for that admonition.

The punchers goaded their horses into the churning waters, shouting and whipping at the milling steers with the hard, wet loops of lariats. The whirlpool of longhorns only grew tighter. At its vortex, Chance saw steers being forced under. Sometimes a head would reappear, but more often than not the animal, once forced under the surface, simply vanished, held under by the churning hooves of the herd.

Billy Joe saw Arlo Smith on a buckskin horse ride against the periphery of the milling cattle and then on into the maw of frantic longhorns. For an instant, it looked as though he might be stemming the swirl of cattle, but in the next moment the rider was torn from his saddle and the buckskin disappeared from view.

Chance spurred the blood bay through the breaking waves of muddy water and through the outer ring of milling cattle. He caught a glimpse of a crumpled black hat and jerked his horse toward it. Then he saw Arlo Smith's head, between a pair of longhorn steers, burst to the surface of the Pecos. His mouth was wide, gasping for breath, and his sparse gray hair was plastered about his eyes.

The loop was already built in Billy Joe's rope. He yelled, "Arlo Smith!" and threw the rope. At the instant the old cowboy grabbed for the loop, another berserk longhorn lunged over him, shoving him beneath the turbid waters.

But Smith had managed to get a hand on the rope. Billy Joe felt the tension. He turned the bay around and rode for the riverbank.

In the shallows he reined up, then drew in the rope. Like a huge catfish just breaking the water's surface, Arlo Smith came toward him. Chance grabbed his shirt collar and the seat of his pants and rolled him out onto the grassy bank.

For the interval of a half-dozen heartbeats, there was no movement from the old puncher. Then he coughed and gagged and a flood of muddy water gushed from his throat. Twice more he retched and spewed forth a stream of river water. Coughing and gasping, he rolled over and sat up, shakily.

Billy Joe watched him until he was breathing regularly. Then, hiding the relief in his voice, he said, "It's a helluva note. The rest of us trying to drive cattle and you're out there taking a swim."

Arlo Smith peeled the long, wet, gray hairs from his eyes, looked at the man on the horse, and swore hoarsely.

"I was doin' fine amongst them longhorns. But you

damn nigh drowned me jerkin' me to shore. I swallered
enough of that water I figgered the river would be dried up
by now.''

"No such luck,'' said Chance. "And we're going to
lose a bunch of 'em if those crazy steers don't come to
their senses.''

Chance was watching the wheeling mass of cattle and
the futile efforts of the drovers to break the mill when he
saw the big, fish-belly steer just beyond the center of the
herd. An idea—a foolish one—surfaced suddenly in his
thoughts.

Instantly, he was off his horse and on the riverbank,
shedding his clothes. Arlo Smith sat watching, speech-
less, until Billy Joe was clad only in pants, boots, and
spurs.

Smith shook his head.

"I guess that swim in the river messed up my brain.
There for a minute I thought you was shuckin' yore
clothes.''

Billy Joe swung back into the saddle on the bay.

"You catch ol' Catamount here when I turn him
loose,'' he said, and reined the horse toward the herd.
Behind him, he heard Arlo Smith shout a question, then
break into a stream of oaths.

The cattle in the gyrating circle were packed more
tightly than ever. He rode against the outer rim, then
stepped off the horse and onto the back of a longhorn.

It was risky going. Walking across the backs of the
wildly thrashing steers was worse than trying to keep his
footing on a floating log in a rushing stream. But the cattle
were packed into a knot, a knot drawn so tightly that he
was able at last to reach the big, cream-colored lead steer.

Chance slid onto the back of the longhorn. The steer,
his eyes rolling wildly, swung his head, trying to reach the
man with the tip of a horn.

On the far bank, Arlo Smith had forgotten that he had
nearly drowned out in that roiling mass of beef. He
watched Chance step nimbly across the herd and take a
seat astride the fish-belly steer. No doubt about it. His
friend had suddenly gone loco, just like the herd of

longhorns trying to destroy themselves out there in the middle of the Pecos River.

But Chance and the steer were moving through the herd, coming toward the bank where Arlo Smith stood. He couldn't see the feet of the cowboy but he knew he was spurring the big steer, guiding him through the maelstrom of crazed, circling cattle.

Gideon Stroop and Whitey and the other drovers had pulled up their horses, too, and were watching the bizarre performance of the young cowboy called Abilene. The steer was coming on, lunging through the other animals, and while they watched he cleared the edge of the herd and his hooves found footing on the sandy bottom of the river. The shirtless puncher on his back kept him moving, until he was out of the water and onto the bank.

And the other three thousand head of longhorns began to peel off from the deadly circle and move toward the bank, too.

The mill was broken.

One by one the longhorns, suddenly bereft of their senseless panic, drifted toward the bank, slaking their thirst and then fighting their way through the bog of the riverbank to begin a search for graze on the flats. In minutes, they were once again a trail herd.

Billy Joe slid from the back of the big lead steer. Arlo Smith came riding on a freshly saddled sorrel, leading Chance's blood bay.

"Was there ever any lunatics in your family, boy?" demanded the older puncher. " 'Cause I believe you caught it, too. That's about the craziest stunt I've ever seen a man pull."

Billy Joe caught the shirt and hat and chaps and gun belt tossed to him by Arlo Smith and began pulling them on.

"Well, I reckon it worked. But I sure would hate to have to ride old Fishbelly plumb to Fort Sumner. He's got a backbone sharper than the blade of a broadax."

They watched Gideon Stroop threading his way through the grazing cattle toward them. His expression was that of a man impaled on the uncomfortable horns of a dilemma.

He reined up and studied Billy Joe a full half-minute while he rolled a cigarette. Then he looked away, his eyes traveling over the loosely scattered herd.

"I'd say we didn't lose over two dozen head. Maybe less."

He stopped, pulled off his hat, and wiped the moisture from the sweatband with a bandanna. Whatever it was he was about to say, it was obvious he wasn't eager to do it.

Then Whitey came out of the herd and rode toward them. Stroop's nervousness grew more pronounced.

Looking at Billy Joe, the straw boss broke the silence.

"That was some show you put on. Waste of time, though. That herd was fixin' to get itself straightened out anyhow." He spat into the grass beside the forefoot of Chance's bay. "Showin' off is about all it amounted to."

He jerked a thumb toward the longhorns.

"You and Smith get to ridin'. We've got a herd to move."

Gideon Stroop spoke then, quietly, with some of the old authority. Once again he was the man in charge.

"Whitey," he said, "you may know about pushin' cows but you don't know beans about pushin' men. I don't think the outfit can afford your bellyachin' ways anymore."

Whitey's colorless brows drew down tight above his deeply sunk eyes.

"Mind telling me what the hell you're talkin' about?"

Stroop pressured the offside of his mount with a spurred boot, moving the horse a step nearer to Whitey.

"You just ain't cuttin' it, pardner. The worst part of this here drive is ahead of us and we need drovers with their minds on movin' longhorns, not a bunch of half-mad punchers with their necks bowed because the straw boss don't know how to give an order."

He paused.

"That's what I'm talkin' about," he said.

Whitey was caught totally off guard. It was more than surprise that was registered in his face. He looked at Stroop, then at Chance and Smith, then back at the trail boss.

"Hell, you can't do that. Old man Pettibone hired me and made me straw boss. And it'll take him to fire me."

Stroop's face was grim.

"I just did. I wouldn't argue with it, was I you."

Whitey knew he was on shaky ground but he wouldn't turn loose.

"You're gonna handle it all by yourself, I suppose," he said. "You'll have a hell of a time doing it."

Then he added, "Unless you've got somebody else in mind for the job."

Stroop inclined his head in a barely perceptible nod.

"I think Abilene there can handle it."

It was the one name out of all the drovers that was the least likely to meet acceptance in the heart of the ex-straw boss. He turned his gaze from Gideon Stroop to Billy Joe and the red in his face turned ashen.

"He'll play hell!" he said. But he couldn't stop there. His next words were meant for Chance.

"I'll drive beef. But I ain't takin' orders from the likes of him. Not for nobody's pay."

The trail boss studied Billy Joe's face.

"What do ya' say? Wanna take the job?"

Billy Joe leaned forward and rested a forearm on his saddlehorn. Arlo Smith could see the half-grin starting on his face.

"I didn't sign on with any ambitions toward helpin' boss a trail herd. But in this case, I think maybe I'll make an exception. Just to see what happens."

Chapter Eight

"**Y**ou ain't gonna like what happens," snapped Whitey, and he jerked his horse about and rode away.

Arlo Smith watched the ex-straw boss's departure.

"I hope you know what you're doin'," he grunted.

"I'll handle it," said Chance.

"Wasn't talkin' to you," said Smith. "I was talkin' to the boss man. He's the one that's gonna be eatin' crow if you mess up."

Stroop ignored the old puncher's observation.

"Abilene, you might as well start earnin' that extra ten bucks a month you're drawin'. We need to get 'em movin'. Those Comanches are likely to come a-callin' again."

Billy Joe was studying the herd, spread out over the broad, grass-covered flat that separated the breaks from the river.

"Since you ask, Mr. Trail Boss," said Chance, "I'll offer a piece of free advice. These here longhorn steers need about three days of standing around in the grass fillin' their bellies and walkin' no more than a hundred yards to soak up that Pecos River water. The Indians aren't likely to make a run at us as long as we're bunched up and every gun is handy."

Stroop looked at Billy Joe for a full half-minute, then he, too, let his eyes wander over the grazing longhorns.

"Could be," he said. "They look like they've got about as much meat on 'em as an overwintered snake."

He motioned to Smith.

"Go break the news to Solomon. We'll be puttin' up here for the next couple of days."

It took only a half-dozen drovers to look after the herd. The rest rode to the bank of the Pecos, shucked their clothes, and slid into the stream. It was the first time they'd seen enough water to bathe in since they'd left Fort Picket nearly a month earlier.

After the splashing and after their clothes had dried, Arlo Smith and Chance rode toward the chuck wagon. The sun was dipping toward the western edge of the world. A few long, big-knuckled clouds lay along the horizon like skinny fingers on a giant hand, reflecting the silver-orange of the setting sun.

"Nice country," said Billy Joe. "No trees to mess up the scenery like there is back in Tennessee."

"Yeah," said Arlo Smith. "And this here river ain't

anything to brag about, either. The only thing good about the Pecos is, it's wet. And it ain't very much of that.''

They rode on a distance in silence.

Finally, Arlo Smith pushed back his hat.

"I'd keep a close eye on that Whitey if I was you, Chance. He's about as mean-tempered as a diamondback. And he sure ain't likely to wanna kiss and make up after you took over his job as straw boss.''

Chance nodded.

"I figure him and me will have some more conversation about that," he said.

He turned and looked at Smith.

"Didn't you tell me he came from someplace in Tennessee?''

"That's right," replied Smith. "Don't rightly know where. Someplace in the hill country you mentioned, as I recollect.''

"What's his name?" asked Chance.

"Whitey's all I ever heard," said the older cowboy.

Billy Joe was silent for a time.

"He's got a funny look," he said at last, thoughtfully. "That white hair and washed-out eyes and all. An albino. Seems like I remember seeing another gent or two with the same look, back in the hills where I grew up.''

Smith worked off a chew of tobacco, then worried it around in his mouth until he got it settled in a cheek.

"Remember that old sodbuster that Stroop hung from the cottonwood when you first come on?" he asked.

Chance nodded.

"Well, that was more Whitey's idea than it was Stroop's," said Smith. "We had some bad stealin' right after we left Fort Picket, and Gid said he'd hang the next man he caught stealin' beef. Well, he didn't figure on it bein' an old, dried-up pilgrim like that, but Whitey kept nippin' at him until he didn't have no other choice.''

"It figures," said Billy Joe.

They were almost to the remuda and the rope corral. Billy Joe's words were casual.

"You're the only gent here who knows my name. Let's keep it that way. Okay?''

"Suits me," said Arlo Smith, and then he chuckled, "There ain't hardly nobody around here that wears his real name except us Smith boys."

With the time to do it, old Solomon had thrown together a son-of-a-gun stew that was, compared to the previously unrelenting diet of beef and beans, mouthwatering. There was considerable palaver among the drovers about the likelihood that Solomon himself had slept through the afternoon and let his youthful swamper prepare the meal, what with it being edible and all.

Solomon growled and drew down his bushy eyebrows and cursed the punchers presently assembled, along with those of past trail drives and those to come. His display of temper only heightened the pleasure the drovers derived from the exchange.

Then Gideon Stroop stepped forward into the circle of firelight. The rattle of voices and the laughter trailed off.

"I've got a little somethin' to tell you boys," said Stroop. "As of right now today, Abilene here will be straw bossin' this outfit. When he gives you an order you just go on and do it like you'd heard it from me. Hear?"

With his words, an instant silence descended on the circle of drovers. Almost as one, they looked along the line of faces opposite. It was Whitey they were looking for.

But Whitey was not among them. Nor was the big puncher, Mule Hunnicutt. And a third man was missing, a sawed-off, quick-tempered puncher who had stopped growing too soon. Shorty was his natural description and his natural handle, but they'd found out quickly enough that he would fight about that nickname. So they chose the opposite extreme by which to address him: Highpockets.

Here and there a grin pulled at the corner of a mouth half-hidden in the shadows of a hat brim. Hardly a puncher among them had not felt the lash of Whitey's temper and tongue. And they were also remembering the fight between Whitey and the man called Abilene. There had been a general absence of sadness among the drovers when Whitey had grabbed the hot iron rod and rendered himself unfit for further combat.

A puncher looked up at Abilene, pushed back his hat, and observed without emotion, "Say, that was some trick you pulled today, Abilene. Gettin' them old steers to break that mill and follow that lead brute out of the river."

Arlo Smith was proud of his friend. It showed in his voice.

"Why, if them old longhorns get tired of walkin', Chance is just liable to have 'em swim right up the Pecos plumb to Fort Sumner."

To a man, they chuckled and nodded. All except Billy Joe. Without intending it, the old man had dropped his name into the conversation.

Chance thought about it, and finally shrugged. The fact that his name was known wasn't likely to make any real difference. If the law was still looking for him for the killing of Newt and Calvin O'Bannon, he had plenty of company. There was a passel of men who had come west for their health, complications that had a great deal more to do with attacks of hempen loops than things like consumption and malaria.

He had left a pack of angry O'Bannons behind after he had sifted lead through the brothers Newt and Calvin, but that had been a half-dozen years ago. The Chance-O'Bannon feud was a thing of the past now, as far as he knew.

Whitey came in to the chuck wagon a half-hour later. With him were Mule Hunnicutt and the fiery-tempered little puncher named Highpockets. They unsaddled and turned their horses in with the remuda and walked toward the chuck wagon. Of the three, Whitey was the only one who stayed outside the faint circle of illumination that radiated weakly outward from the firelight.

"Well, it's cold," said the cook, Solomon. "I cain't keep no meal hot all night while you jaspers 'er out lookin' at the countryside. You're lucky I didn't throw it out for the coyotes to eat."

"Shut up."

It was Whitey's voice from the darkness at the rear of the wagon. His tone had the rasping unpleasantness of a crosscut saw pinched in a shifting log.

Hunnicutt and the puncher named Highpockets came with their tin plates and sat down at the edge of the firelight. Whitey was somewhere back in the deeper shadows.

The conversation among the other drovers had tapered off. They knew Whitey's temperament and they knew it wouldn't take but one wrong word to set off a first-class explosion that would likely prove unwholesome for any gent who happened to be loitering close by.

Gideon Stroop appeared oblivious to the flash point of tension that hung in the air. He knelt at the fire, withdrew a burning twig of cedar, and ignited his cigarette.

"We'll give them old longhorns a couple more days to fatten up enough so's they'll at least cast a shadow, and then we'll head 'em north." He drew in a lungful of smoke and blew out the residue. "We're lucky we've still got enough beef to call a trail herd after they went loco and started that mill in the river today."

Billy Joe was trying to keep an eye on Whitey, who was little more than a vague outline in the dimness beside the chuck wagon. It wasn't Whitey who spoke now, though. It was Highpockets. His voice from the far rim of firelight was cold and hard, the brittle hardness of a pond's surface in the dead of winter.

"That was pure horse manure, showin' off with that ol' fish-belly steer."

Highpockets's eyes moved up and found Whitey in the darkness, then returned to the plate in his hands. He stood, walked to the black, steaming pot beside the fire, and dropped the tin into the water.

The absence of sound among the circle of drovers intensified. Billy Joe stood without moving and rolled himself a cigarette. He'd expected trouble, but he had expected it to come from Whitey or Mule Hunnicutt, not from the little puncher called Highpockets. It was a cinch bet, though, that it was Whitey who'd set him on the prod.

But Billy Joe let the cowboy's challenge hang there. There wasn't any danger of gunfire spooking the herd of longhorns, but neither was there any point in shooting a man to demonstrate that he was, indeed, the second in command now.

Highpockets had made his decision, however. He was going to push it. Whether it was to prove something to Whitey or whether it was simply the problem of a little man with a big Colt on his hip wasn't clear to Billy Joe. But where it was all heading was fairly obvious.

"I said the gent that put on the show out in the river was showin' off. We'd a had that herd unwound in another little bit."

He hitched up his gun belt. It was an unconscious gesture but Chance recognized in it the movement of a man who had handled a Colt more than he had a fork and a spoon.

Still he said nothing. He didn't want it to end in a shooting. A straw boss who had to gun his way through his men wasn't worthy of the name.

Highpockets read something else into Billy Joe's silence. He looked up into the face of the other man, then spat between his teeth into the coals of the fire. His words were intended for the rest of the drovers but his eyes remained on Chance's face.

"I ain't about to take orders from no fancy-dan straw boss who wasn't even around when the drive started. Hell, we don't know nothing about this jasper. He comes ridin' up out of nowhere and signs on without so much as a by-yore-leave to anybody."

He pushed back his hat and stood with his thumbs hooked in his cartridge belt. Billy Joe sighed. The other man was backing himself into a corner where gunplay was the only way out.

Chance dropped his cigarette butt in the coals.

"Just back off and let it lay right there," he said gently.

Highpockets was working himself into the proper mood. It showed in his eyes, in the manner in which his mouth was drawn down, and in the way his feet were spread and braced.

"Well, if that ain't one hell of a note," he said, too loud. "I'd say this here Injun fighter ain't near as mean as he tries to look."

Billy Joe sent a glance toward Whitey. That puncher

had moved forward until the light broke on his face. In his eyes shone an eager, hungry look, the kind a lobo wolf was likely to wear while he eased in on a crippled calf.

A few steps from him stood Arlo Smith. Billy Joe's gaze touched him briefly and he saw reassurance in Smith's eyes. The old cowboy would make sure that the fight, if it came to that, was a fair one.

Gideon Stroop had said nothing and Billy Joe didn't expect him to. Stroop was waiting to see if his new straw boss had enough sand in his craw to handle the job.

Chance looked back at the other puncher. A straw boss ought to worry first about the herd.

"Tell you what, Highpockets. Let it go till we get these old longhorns to Fort Sumner. Then we'll settle her anyway you want to."

Highpockets laughed, a high-pitched squeak that sounded much like a giggle. He knew it and it quickened his wrath.

"No, I'll tell you what, fancy dan. We'll settle it right here and now. There's one of us ain't gonna see the likes of Fort Sumner. Ever."

Gideon Stroop knew then that it had gone farther than he had intended. He moved away from the wheel of the chuck wagon and into the circle of firelight.

"That's enough, High," he said. "You've made your point. Now drop it. It was my idea to move him up to straw boss, and I'm still callin' the shots."

Highpockets didn't take his eyes from Billy Joe's face.

"This is between him and me. You're out."

Highpockets was wound too tightly. Stroop opened his mouth and started to lift his hand. It was that movement that touched off the nerves in the brain and the hand of the stunted puncher.

Billy Joe Chance saw it coming. He read it in the face of Highpockets and he knew when the other man's reflexes passed the point of no return.

The short man was fast. His six-gun had cleared leather and was swinging up when the two hundred grains of lead from Billy Joe's Colt collided with his breastbone at about the third button of his shirt. Highpockets's thumb slipped from the hammer of his gun and the bullet punched a pair of holes in the coffeepot resting at the edge of the fire.

The escaping coffee hissed against the coals as the sound of the explosions died away. The little cowboy, his hand still trying feebly to cock the hammer again, slid to his knees and then folded forward onto his face.

At daybreak, they wrapped the stunted drover in his bedroll, lashed it tight with the rope that hung from the hornstring of his saddle, and scooped out a shallow grave beneath the rim of the high ground away from the river. Billy Joe stood off from the other men with his hat in his hand and watched the new day pour a red-gold gloss over the breaks that bound the Pecos River.

Chapter Nine

Even the longhorns were anxious to be on the move. With the fish-belly steer stretching out proud in the lead, they struck a quick gait and began the long march to Fort Sumner, where the army still needed beef even though the dread Bosque Redondo Reservation no longer held its thousands of miserable redskin captives.

For days they trailed north, with trouble keeping its distance. Then the wind came.

At first it was of little consequence, a nudging south-westerly breeze that was hardly more than a zephyr. But on the second day it grew in intensity, viciously. By early afternoon of that day it was snatching up pebbles and hurling them at the drovers and the animals with stinging velocity. A hat negligently unsecured with a latch beneath the chin was lost forever. Weeds and bits of grass and leaves left over from winter rode the rising wind in waves like swarms of gnats.

But worst of all was the dust.

For once the drag men, the cowboys at the tail end of the herd, didn't have to eat it all. The alkali dust chopped into powder with the passing of the three thousand cattle was whipped away the instant a hoof struck the earth. The men at the point and those along the flanks of the half-mile-long line of march took a breath carefully, and only when they had to. Neckerchiefs covered mouths and noses, and hats were screwed down until their owners' ears stood out from their heads.

Night gave no relief from the pounding, whipping wind. Solomon tried to build a fire in the lee of a cutbank but gave it up after he had used half the supply of matches remaining in the chuck box. The drovers made their meal of gritty jerky, cold biscuits, and the bitter, cathartic water of the Pecos River.

Billy Joe was saddling a fresh horse when Gideon Stroop rode up and stepped down.

He wiped at his eyes a moment.

"Hell, I don't remember old man Goodnight or anybody else talkin' about havin' to drive through a cyclone up this trail."

At the rear of the chuck wagon a dozen paces away, Solomon was upending an iron pot. Dust poured from the vessel and was instantly caught and whirled away by the wind.

"Helluva note," he snapped, having to shout to be heard above the whistling of the wind. "Cain't build a fire. Cain't make coffee. Hell, a man cain't even light a cigarette. I ain't had one since yestiddy morning."

Arlo Smith, trailed by a freshly saddled claybank gelding, grinned through his dust-caked beard, white now instead of gray because of its alkali encrustment.

"You fellers oughta give up them smokes and take up chawin' tobaccy. Don't need no matches to get it going. And a man don't have to worry about startin' prairie fires and such."

Billy Joe grunted a mild oath.

"Maybe not. But I sure know a gent who needs to be more careful about what's downwind of him before he takes and unloads a mouthful of tobacco juice. Dang me if

I don't believe I'd rather be downwind of a scoured-up dogie calf.''

Arlo Smith wiped at his mouth with the stained sleeve of his shirt.

"A little tobaccy juice ain't never hurt nobody. It's good for a lot of things, too. Snakebite, boils, bad temper . . .''

Stroop pulled his hat down tighter.

"We'll make the crossing back to the other side of the river when we hit the mouth of the Delaware *mañana*. That oughta cut down on the dust some."

They made the crossing before noon the following day, but Stroop failed in his prediction. The wind and dust continued unabated. The steers felt the ill temper of the drovers and were uneasy. When Stroop called a halt at sundown, the longhorns milled for hours, restlessly.

Then the Comanches struck.

It was an hour before first light, perhaps, when the wind that had plagued them for three days became suddenly remorseful and slunk away. Almost instantly, the steers settled in and forgot their uneasiness.

A bit of gray was beginning to show along the eastern horizon. For the drovers on final nightguard, it was a good time. Alabama Pete pulled his neckerchief down from his face and crowded his hat to the back of his head.

He looked over at another horseman, a drover named T.Z. Riggs, and grinned, sending cracks through the mask of alkali dust that had crept under his kerchief.

"Hey, T., didn't I tell you the wind would quit today? Didn't I?''

Riggs grinned back and shook his head.

"Naw, that ain't what you said, Pete. What you said was, 'Any fool that would watch a steer's rear end across five hundred miles of desert when he could be layin' under a tree alongside a crick with a fishin' pole in his hand oughta have his head unscrewed and washed out with lye soap.' That's what you said, as I recollect.''

Alabama Pete chuckled.

"Well, maybe I did mention that little crick back of my pa's place. And them honeysuckles in the spring turning the air sweeter'n a pretty girl's breath.''

He sighed and shifted onto one hip in his saddle.

"When this here drive is over, I'm gonna go back and see if the old place still looks the same. Dang me if I ain't."

Then a bullet from a Comanche rifle jerked Alabama Pete from his saddle and into eternity.

Instantly, before the sound of the shot had faded, the shrieks of two score Comanche braves rent the stillness of the morning. They came boiling down from the rim of the cap rock in a wave of terrible fury. The herd of longhorns, so recently reduced to calm, fetched themselves to their feet and broke into a fragmented, frantic run.

Chapter Ten

Scattered in random fashion on the ground around the chuck wagon were the bedrolls of the off-duty drovers. Some had already begun to stir awake as the false dawn lightened the sky. Most, though, were still asleep, enjoying for the first time in three days the ecstasy of rest undisturbed by a howling wind and breathing made painful by a dust-laden atmosphere.

Billy Joe Chance was one of the former. He had his boots and his gun belt in place and was pulling on his hat when the first shot sounded. Close at hand was the black horse he had saddled and hobbled at the tail end of the preceding day.

Now, he sprang into the saddle, still unable to discern in the half-light the magnitude of the attack. But he could see, in the bedroll a few feet from his own, a young drover fighting to get free of his blankets. In the haze of sudden wakefulness, habit guided the young cowboy's actions. The first thing he reached for was his hat.

It was his last. Still on his knees on the bedroll, he

jerked stiffly upward. Then he slid forward, face down, and lay still.

Other punchers, those with night mounts still saddled, were scrambling into their saddles. To the nearest ones, Chance shouted, "They'll be after the horses," and then he broke in a run toward the remuda. A minute later, looking back, he recognized the rider a few strides behind him—the ex-straw boss, Whitey.

"This is your doin', Chance," shouted Whitey. "They're payin' us back for what you did."

Billy Joe looked into the twisted face of Whitey and saw there something more than the remnants of a grudge. It was hate, a bitter, personal kind of hate.

He turned to the front, saw a Comanche on a racing horse closing in on the remuda, and shot him from the saddle with his Winchester. He had time to ponder for no more than an instant the fact that Whitey had called him by name—Chance. Then a pair of warriors was coming at him from the ravine that split the bluffs.

He shot once, missed, shot again, and saw where the bullet hit. It struck the Indian's horse in the neck and the animal turned a cartwheel, spilling the Comanche into the buffalo grass beneath the tumbling half-ton of paint pony.

The remaining Indian was coming up fast. Chance levered another cartridge into the Winchester and at the same instant heard a rifle explode directly behind him. He heard the bullet slap the air beside his ear and glanced over his shoulder.

Whitey was a horse's length behind him and bringing his rifle up again. Whether by accident or design, his first shot had been inches from Billy Joe's ear. Chance reined his running mount out of the line of fire, shifted the Winchester to his other hand, and drew his Colt.

The third warrior was close now, close enough that Chance could see the string of eagles' talons strung about his neck. It was for that target that he aimed. The Indian slumped across the withers of his horse and then slid in a cartwheeling heap to the ground beneath the racing hooves of his pony.

But the shouting and shooting had spooked the remuda. In a squealing, kicking stampede, the hundred and some cow ponies swept through the rope barrier and broke for freedom.

Instantly, Billy Joe made his decision. The horses would have to wait. The sound of gunfire and bawling longhorns was rattling against the bluffs behind him.

He wanted on top of those bluffs with his Winchester. He shot a quick glance over his shoulder. Whitey was no longer in sight. He sent the black horse scrambling up the steep wall of the escarpment.

At the summit, he turned and sped along the uneven, boulder-strewn rim of the cliff until he was at a point almost directly above the battle that was raging between the drovers and the war party of Comanches. Like the horses, the frightened steers had exploded into a stampede as the first gunshots had sounded. Now the cowboys were falling back, seeking cover along the ragged dropoff that bordered the river.

As Chance watched, a hatless, balding puncher slid from his horse and dived for the sandy embankment at the water's edge. Then, inexplicably, he stood up and turned halfway around. It was as though he wanted one more look at the field of battle.

But even from the remoteness of the bluffs, Chance could see the bright eruption of blood on his chest. A Comanche bullet had struck him between the shoulder blades and exited about where his heart would have been.

The puncher toppled over backward, struck the water with a great splash, and sank beneath the spinning, sand-red current of the Pecos.

Billy Joe sprang from his saddle, tore open a saddle-bag, and drew from it a sock full of Winchester cartridges. Beneath him, among the boulders at the base of the bluffs, the Comanches were regrouping for another assault against the thin line of drovers backed up against the river's edge.

Chance dropped to the ground, reloaded the repeating rifle, and drew a bead on the bronzed back of a Comanche warrior.

He got off seven shots before the Indians understood that the shots were coming not from in front of them but from above. And with those seven shots, Chance put seven Comanches out of the fighting. Not all of them were dead, but all of them had lost immediate interest in trying to kill Texas drovers.

The Indians had their flank badly exposed. The only wise thing to do was to beat a retreat, and they did it in haste. Two more fell to bullets from Gideon Stroop's cowboys before they had crowded their ponies through the maze of boulders and up a brush-choked ravine to the safety of the high mesa.

Billy Joe mounted and sent the black gelding down the near-vertical face of the bluff. A shower of sandstones and red earth followed him to the litter of boulders that bordered the flats below. Three Comanches were still alive. One was struggling to swing his rifle about when Billy Joe shot him in the chest. The other two were barely alive.

He rode on to the point near the river where the cowboys, some on horseback and some on foot, were gathering.

To a puncher without a shirt and boots, one of those who had been caught in a deep sleep by the sudden attack, he said, "Go kill those two Indians that are still breathing."

A trio of drovers on horseback came toward him. One was Whitey and another was Mule Hunnicutt. The third was a Negro cowboy named Ivy Spurlin.

"Let's get after those horses," he ordered.

Abruptly he stopped and looked at the faces around him, taking quick inventory.

"Where's Stroop?"

Arlo Smith, hatless and horseless, was reloading his Winchester. He looked around, frowning.

"I seen him right after them Injuns hit, Billy Joe," he said. "He was makin' for cover right over yonder. On foot."

Downriver the four riders went, following the tracks and the haze of dust left behind by the fugitive remuda. A quarter-mile away they came to a gentler slope that led to the flat tableland of prairie above. Up it they rode, and kept their horses in a run, paralleling the river and the course of the runaways.

Another mile and they saw the remuda, their urge to run to the end of the world already fading. The four horsemen circled away from the lip of the bluff and out of sight of the horses, rode another half-mile downstream, and swung back toward the river. In minutes, they had the remuda gathered up and headed north.

Ivy Spurlin swung his horse in beside Billy Joe's.

"I ain't for certain but I suspicion we're shy a few head," he said. "I don't see that Pretty Boy hoss of mine and I know there's a couple others missin'."

Billy Joe nodded.

"Yep. Maybe ten or a dozen. Likely they cut out over the bluffs when they went to running. I'd guess they'll end up in some Comanche's string."

The rope corral was up when they reached the chuck wagon and the other drovers. They turned the remuda in and Billy Joe rode to the wagon. In the shade of it, on a bedroll, lay Gideon Stroop. The cook and Arlo Smith were kneeling at his side.

"What happened?" asked Chance.

"Took one about here," said Smith, jabbing a thumb against his chest. "Looks pretty bad."

Stroop coughed, and a froth of blood bubbled at the corner of his mouth.

"Through his lung," said Billy Joe.

"Ain't bleedin' too bad, unless it's inside," said Solomon.

"How many others?"

"Roaney got it 'fore he ever got out of his bedroll," said Arlo Smith. "And Candy Tom ain't been found. Don't know what happened to him."

"Look downriver a ways," said Chance. "He went into the water. I saw it. But he was already dead."

Stroop's eyes opened, and he looked around wildly for a moment and tried to sit up. Solomon held his shoulders to the ground. Slowly his senses returned.

"Chance," he said, and the words were barely a whisper. "It's yours now."

"Sure, Gid," said Billy Joe. "We'll put you in the

wagon. You'll live to have yourself a couple of drinks at Fort Sumner."

He turned away. If his last statement wasn't a lie, there wasn't anybody who'd be more surprised than he.

They found Candy Tom a hundred yards downriver. One spurred boot had caught in a tangle of saltbush limbs at the water's edge. But what Billy Joe saw first in the bitter waters of the Pecos was a ribbon of crimson mingling with the twisting, sand-shot current—crimson that spilled from the great wound in Candy Tom's chest.

They buried Roaney and Candy Tom and Alabama Pete in a shallow grave, unmarked, beneath the bluffs, then pried loose boulders to seal the graves and ensure that the three drovers' final rest would be undisturbed by badgers, coyotes, or Comanches.

Chance looked beneath the canvas cover that had been rigged above the hoodlum wagon and saw that Gideon Stroop had lapsed into a fitful sleep. He turned and summoned Arlo Smith with a crook of his hand.

"Get the boys together," said Billy Joe.

They gathered there in the blood-crusted sand along the bank of the Pecos, their numbers already reduced by a fourth and the Bosque Redondo yet two hundred miles away.

Billy Joe sat his horse and looked over the handful of cowboys. What was it? Barely a month ago, when he had set out simply to find a puncher's job of driving longhorns? Now, misfortune and Comanche lead had thrown the responsibility of trail boss into his hands. He'd never done it, nor had the desire to.

But when he spoke his voice was matter-of-fact.

"Stroop's hurt bad. That leaves me runnin' this lashup. Those of you who don't like the idea can get your warbag and ride on out. There'll be no hard feelin's. I'll write you a letter so you can draw your wages."

He paused and scanned the faces in the semicircle before him.

"If you stay on, you'll do it my way."

There was silence for a full half-minute. Then Ivy Spurlin cleared his throat.

"Is they gonna be a straw boss, Mr. Chance?"

Billy Joe let his eyes wander across the gathering of punchers.

"If there's straw bossin' to be done, Arlo Smith will handle it."

He wasn't watching Smith. His gaze was on the face of Whitey, standing a half-dozen paces away from the others. The eyes of the ex-straw boss were hard, venomous. Chance saw his lips form an oath, but if he spoke, the sound wasn't loud enough to be heard.

"Okay," said Chance. "That's it. There's three thousand head of longhorns runnin' loose up the river. Fork your horses and get to movin'."

He sent the black into motion but another rider swung in beside him.

"I ain't doin' it. I ain't takin' the job. I ain't never been a straw boss or any other kind of boss and I ain't fixin' to start now," said Arlo Smith.

Billy Joe looked across at him and nodded and grinned a tight grin.

"I appreciate your volunteerin', Mr. Smith. I figured I could count on you in a pinch. But I don't want you chousin' the boys too hard. Just you remember what happened to ol' Whitey when his authority went to his head."

Arlo Smith broke into a string of oaths that ended only when he had to discharge a mouthful of tobacco juice.

"You ain't heerd a word I said," he shouted, but Billy Joe had gigged his horse into a run and was quickly out of earshot.

Billy Joe's hopes of finding the longhorns bunched on the flats along the river died abruptly. The stampeding herd had split, and split again, in its mad dash away from the terrifying sounds of the daybreak battle.

He sent punchers in pairs up the slopes of the cap rock to collect the several fragments of the herd that had headed for the bald prairie. He wasn't worried that the Comanches would be looking to gather in the steers. Unless they had opportunity to trade cattle to the Comancheros, they weren't much interested in beef. Horses for riding and horsemeat for eating were where their appetites lay.

It was after sundown when the last drovers came in with another handful of longhorns and threw them into the bobtailed herd. Chance started toward the hoodlum wagon when Arlo Smith rode in.

"I want the night guard doubled," said Billy Joe. "See to it."

Arlo Smith aimed a finger, crooked into a knotted angle by too many dallies of the lariat around his saddlehorn.

"I told you this mornin' and I'm tellin' you ag'in. I ain't cut out to boss nothin' except them empty-headed longhorns and maybe a stubborn bronc or such. Don't go tellin' me what orders to give, 'cause I . . ."

"See to it," said Billy Joe, and turned on his heel.

Arlo Smith reined his horse about with a jerk that made the animal rear and pivot on his hind legs.

"Damn hardheaded, wet-eared kid," he muttered in his beard. "Won't listen to nothin' 'er nobody. I'm beginnin' to savvy how come them O'Bannons got theirselves into a feud with that bunch."

Billy Joe watched him ride away and grinned. He had read Arlo Smith right. The old puncher would complain bitterly but he would be loyal to his last breath. And Billy Joe figured he'd need every ounce of loyalty he could put his hands on before the herd reached its destination.

Inside the hoodlum wagon, the heat was intense even though the canvas sheet was tied up around the edges. Gideon Stroop's features were ashen. He looked into Billy Joe's face and attempted a grin. It failed.

"Get 'em gathered in?" His voice was thin. The words came with an effort.

Chance shook his head.

"Less than half. We'll be a couple of days yet." He nodded toward the cook. "Solomon takin' proper care of you?" This time the trail boss managed the grin. "I'd-a had better doctorin' if you'd left me back there with the Injuns. He thinks horse liniment is supposed to cure anything."

Solomon was rummaging through a sack of paraphernalia, a frown clouding his face.

"Whatever kind of medicine you're feedin' him, just keep on with it," said Chance.

"Don't you worry yore *cabeza* none about Mr. Stroop here," growled the cook. "I'll look after him. You tend to yore own knittin'."

Billy Joe stepped down and started to turn away. The whispering voice of Gideon Stroop drew him back to the wagon.

"Watch yourself," said the trail boss, focusing his eyes on Billy Joe's face with an effort. "There's trouble in the makin'."

"It's gonna be okay," said Billy Joe. "We're gonna get through."

Stroop's eyes closed as though from overpowering weariness. Slowly he shook his head. His eyes opened with an effort.

"I ain't talkin' about the herd. I'm talkin' about . . ."

The sentence remained uncompleted. Billy Joe waited a full half-minute. Then he said, "You're talking about the hands?"

Stroop's mouth was half-open. Saliva, showing a pink trace of blood, ran across his cheek to his ear. Billy Joe bent lower. The word was not spoken but it was formed on the lips of the trail boss.

"Whitey!"

Billy Joe read it clearly and it stayed in his thoughts as he mounted and rode his horse to the wranglers' nighttime corral.

Chapter Eleven

The night guard was doubled and the punchers in their bedrolls slept so lightly that a waterbug skating on a

backwater eddy would have awakened them. But the
Comanches didn't come. At the end of the second day, the
wagons had moved northward along the Pecos for a dozen
miles and, little by little, the herd had grown as hard-
riding punchers gathered the steers from brushy draws.

The late afternoon sun was softening the harsh shades
of prairie gold and spilling shadows into the depths of the
river canyon. In the distance, westward, the purple-hued
Guadalupe Mountains rose ominously above the plain.

Billy Joe and Arlo Smith sat their horses side by side
on the rim overlooking the flats that bordered the Pecos.
The sounds of shouting drovers and the occasional lonesome bawling of a longhorn steer troubled by a vague
sense of the time when he had had the accoutrements of a
bull issued up to them on the cooling, rising air.

"I'd say we ain't lost more'n a couple hundred," said
Smith.

"You're close," said Chance. "But we're not going
to spend any more time ridin' out these draws. We're
headin' north at first light with the bunch we have."

Arlo Smith drew a jackknife, its blade black from
previous cuttings, sliced a corner from a plug of chewing
tobacco, and packed it into his jaw.

"How does Stroop look? What's his chances?"

"Slim to none," said Billy Joe. "I'd rather draw to
an inside straight as bet he'll be alive when we reach
Sumner."

He paused for a time.

"He told me to watch for trouble. From Whitey. That
mean anything to you?"

Smith studied the line where the earth and sky met in
the distance for a long interval, then spat into the buffalo
grass.

"Don't reckon I know what Stroop was talkin' about
partic'larly, but in general I'd have to agree. Whitey ain't
got over you takin' his place as straw boss. And now
you're runnin' the whole outfit. It ain't likely to improve
his disposition."

Billy Joe started to speak, but Arlo Smith broke in
and the tone of his voice stopped Chance abruptly.

"That ain't all Whitey has ag'in you, Billy Joe. There's somethin' else stickin' in his craw, but dadblame me if I can figure it out. It's like he's been workin' up a dislike for you for a long time. You ever meet up with him afore you signed on with this outfit?"

Chance's gaze was on the horizon, too, and his mind was only half on his answer.

"Nope, don't reckon so," he said.

He pointed to the east, away from the setting sun, toward a gentle fold in the prairie.

"You see that rise yonder? Keep your eyes on it a minute and tell me what you see."

Arlo Smith followed the pointing finger and squinted his eyes in the failing light.

"Nothin'. I don't see a danged thing except a couple hundred miles of rawhide-dry country that we drove these sweet-natured longhorns over. You're imaginin' things."

"Well, you look again," said Chance.

Smith looked, started to turn back, then jerked his gaze eastward again.

"Yeah. You're right as rain. Somethin's movin' there. Just topping that rise." He was already reaching for the Winchester in the saddle boot beneath his knee. "That same bunch of Comanches, I'd say. Lookin' to finish off what they started three days ago."

"Naw. Your eyes are givin' out on you," said Chance. "That's not riders. That's a wagon of some sort."

He pulled about the stocking-legged sorrel he was riding.

"Think I'll take a look-see. Can't imagine what a wagonload of folks would be doing out here in Comanche country by themselves."

"I'm the straw boss of this outfit. You said so yourself," snorted Smith. "Guess I'd best ride along and see to it you stay out of trouble."

The blue of daylight was fast disappearing by the time they came within hailing distance of the wagon. Billy Joe called out and saw an arm signal an answer. He and Arlo Smith rode on in.

Hitched to the covered wagon was a pair of brindle

oxen, big, rawboned creatures that looked as though they had walked without stopping from the Concho River breaks.

The condition of the wagon was no better. The off drive wheel needed greasing. They could hear it squall while they were still a quarter-mile away. A water barrel fixed to the side of the wagon was obviously empty. Daylight, what there was remaining, showed between the dry, shrunken staves.

The wagon drew to a lurching halt as the two horsemen approached.

"Howdy," said Billy Joe, his hand going to the brim of his hat.

He wasn't prepared for what he saw.

The man sitting on the seat of the worn wagon wouldn't have looked much worse if he'd been three days dead. His eyes were sunken so deeply beneath his heavily browed forehead that they were nothing but two pools of shadow. His face was drawn and sunken too, with the gaunt look of one of those thirst-crazed longhorns that had died in their tracks during the last ten miles to the water of the Pecos River.

"Howdy," repeated Billy Joe.

The man on the seat reached up a hand to tilt his hat brim, but the hand never made it. It was as though the effort drained the last ounce of strength from his trembling arm.

"Howdy," he replied. His voice was parched and dry, like the wheel that had sent its greaseless squeal of protest across the plains.

"Where you bound?" asked Chance.

"Santa Fe," came the brittle response.

"Where from?"

The man on the wagon seat hooked a thumb over his shoulder.

"Rawlsville."

Arlo Smith crowded his horse nearer.

"Rawlsville? You don't mean to say you come all the way from Rawlsville?"

The wagon driver nodded tiredly.

"There ain't nothin' between there and here," said

Smith. "Nothin' exceptin' Injuns. There sure ain't any water. A buffalo waller or two, maybe."

"Only one," said the man, his voice cracking.

He looked at Billy Joe.

"Are we headed for Horsehead Crossing?"

Chance shook his head.

"Nope. You're not even in Texas. You're in the territory."

The man looked about him wildly for a moment.

"I was aimin' for Horsehead."

"You missed it a mite. About two weeks' traveling time, I'd judge," said Chance.

With a lean, bony arm, the man on the wagon seat pushed back his dusty black hat and wiped the moisture from his forehead with a galloused sleeve that once had been passably white.

"Name's Phike," he said suddenly, swallowing so that his Adam's apple sprang suddenly into motion and then vanished in the gray-black nest of hair at the V of his collarless shirt. "Will Phike."

It was said almost supplicatingly, and Billy Joe saw that the sunken eyes were fixed on the leather-pouched canteen at his saddlehorn. Will Phike was offering all he had, the unreserved gift of his name, for the contents of that canteen.

"How long's it been since you had water?" he asked.

"We ran out a ways back."

"How long?" echoed Arlo Smith.

"Three days."

Chance unstrung his canteen and, leaning from his saddle, handed it to the man on the wagon. He pulled the stopper and they both saw him lick his parched, cracked lips. But instead of taking a drink he leaned and handed the canteen back through the puckered mouth of canvas into the depths of the covered wagon.

The two horsemen heard a weak cry. There was movement within the wagon, and whimpering, and the sound of the water sloshing in the canteen.

Billy Joe reached over, took the canteen that hung

suspended from the swell of Arlo Smith's saddle, and passed it across to the man on the wagon.

"You've got family?"

Will Phike nodded, but his eyes were on the canteen. He put it to his mouth and drank a long swallow. Then he took it down and put the stopper back in the neck. The effort it cost him to take only that one swallow was mirrored in his eyes, and it was a painful thing to see.

He extended the canteen toward Billy Joe.

Chance shook his head.

"Have all you want."

Phike drank again, then turned and spoke into the opening behind him.

"Martha. Come up here."

A woman appeared at the mouth of canvas. Close behind her came a towheaded boy of seven, perhaps eight. And the last to emerge from the depths of the emigrant wagon was a slender reed of a girl, so small and delicate that Billy Joe at first took her for a child, hardly older than the boy. But then she came farther into the light of dusk and he realized she was older, but still a year or two short of twenty.

Like the man, the two women and the boy were hollow-eyed, their lips cracked and bleeding. The boy was still sucking at the mouth of the canteen, even though all the water was gone from it.

The old man's voice was clearer now.

"These are the folks who give us the water. You children mind your manners."

The boy looked at the two mounted men and smiled with a broad smile that lacked a full contingent of teeth.

"It sure tasted good," said the boy. "Thanks a heap."

The girl's eyes traveled to Billy Joe, then to Arlo Smith, and quickly back to Chance. It was only the briefest of looks and, on the surface, timid and reserved. But within that gaze was a strength that contained pride and a hint of challenge. He knew in that instant that life wouldn't conquer her without a battle.

"I'm grateful to you. Both," came the girl's voice. It

hadn't been used much in recent days, thought Chance. It had almost the deep resonance of a man's voice.

Martha Phike was a woman who would have been obese under more favorable circumstances. Now she smiled through cracked lips and nodded.

"You've saved our lives. That's what you've done," she said.

But Will Phike wasn't ready to concede that. He wasn't ready to quit. Suddenly, Billy Joe saw deeper into the man and his respect for the wayward emigrant grew.

"We'd have made it," said Will Phike to his wife.

He turned back to Chance.

"How far?" he asked with intensity. "How far to the river?"

"Five miles. No more," said Arlo Smith. "You'd-a made it, all right. That is, if you'd-a leaned west just a shade more."

Phike shook his head, like a man listening to his own thoughts.

"We'd have made it," he said stonily.

Arlo Smith was curious.

"How come you folks to head this direction? Horsehead Crossing is about due west of Rawlsville."

Will Phike's face, seamed and rasped with sun and windblown sand, became crimson beneath its coat of brown.

"We just drifted off the trail, I guess," said he.

"Now, Will," said his wife. "Go ahead and tell them. It won't make it any worse."

Phike turned and cast a flinty look at Martha, but then he turned back to the two horsemen.

"There was a man. There at the post where we outfitted. He said he knew a shorter trail to Santa Fe. One with plenty of water." He ducked his head, looking down at his shoes. "He was going to guide us through but he left the second night. Just disappeared during the night."

He cleared his throat.

"We thought for a while that maybe the Indians had got him."

Billy Joe looked away, to save the old man embarrassment and to conceal the curl of his lips. Will Phike was far from being the first emigrant to fall for such dupery. And he had survived it. Many hadn't.

Abruptly the shrill voice of the boy broke into his thoughts.

"Pa had to give him money, too. A whole lot . . ."

Will Phike turned on the seat and grabbed the ear of the boy, twisting it until a squeal of pain escaped from the lad's cracked lips.

"You hush your mouth, Sidney!" said the man.

Sidney immediately fell silent and sank to the sideboard of the wagon, rubbing his reddened ear.

Arlo Smith was studying the gaunt pair of oxen hitched to the wagon.

"That's sort of a queer thing," he said to Phike. "Don't believe I've ever seen a pair as bobtailed as them two."

Chance followed his gaze. The tails of both steers were only stubs, hardly longer than a man's thumb.

Will Phike rubbed a hand against his bearded face.

"Yeah. Well, we ran short of grub." Despite himself, it seemed, he glanced toward his wife. "There wasn't nothin' else to eat."

"We biled 'em," said Sidney. "And we et 'em."

Billy Joe motioned with his hand.

"You folks are welcome at the chuck wagon. Solomon isn't the best cook that's ever gone up the trail, but it won't kill you."

Will Phike's neck stiffened noticeably.

"Much obliged," he said. "But we'll be movin' on. Do thank you for the water."

Timidly, hesitantly, his wife spoke.

"Will," she said, almost with apology. "Don't you think we could stop with them for just a bit? The children need something to eat."

Phike turned on her and spoke sharply.

"We're not takin' no handouts, Martha."

Sidney said, "Please, pa. I'm hungry."

Without looking at his son, Phike said, "Boy, I don't want to hear any more out of you."

And then there was silence. It angered Billy Joe. The man's pride was going to get them killed yet. How they had managed to cross the cruel vastness of the Llano without starving to death or, worse, falling into the hands of the Comanches or a gang of Comanchero traders, was nothing short of a miracle.

But it wasn't his lookout. He reined his horse away, ready to signal Arlo Smith that it was time to leave. But then the girl spoke. There was neither hesitancy nor apology in her tone. She said it matter-of-factly:

"Mister, if you think it won't put you out, we'd be mighty pleased to accept your offer."

"Now, Charity, I won't have it. . . ."

Will Phike's voice trailed off. Billy Joe couldn't tell if it was the girl's purposefulness or her father's own sudden good sense that wrought the change. But at last Phike nodded.

"Much obliged," he said, grudgingly.

Chance and Smith rode ahead, accommodating the pace of their horses to the snaillike tread of the tailless oxen of Will Phike. All that was left of daylight was a faint trace of translucent blue against the long, unbroken line of the western horizon.

Arlo Smith glanced over his shoulder at the wagon, the white roundness of its top jerking and swaying in the semidarkness.

"I cain't believe a growed man would set out to cross the Llano like that. With his family and all," he said. "If that ain't a good way to get your hair lifted I don't know what is."

Billy Joe grunted.

"Another day or so without water and they wouldn't have cared."

They rode in silence for a time, the squeal of the ungreased hub on the wagon behind them splintering the quiet of the prairie night.

"She's probably the reason they got as far as they did."

"She who?" asked Smith.

"The girl."

"What about her?"

"I'd bet she's the one that held the outfit together. It was probably her idea to eat the tails off those two steers."

Even though it was too dark to see anything more than an outline, Arlo Smith turned and gazed for some time at the man on the horse beside him.

"Well, now," he said, drawing the words out. "Sounds to me like you've give that some serious thought. That skinny little gal already gettin' under your skin?"

Billy Joe swore.

"If it wasn't so dark and you weren't so goldanged old, I'd get off right here and relieve you of them two or three teeth you have left. All I said was, that girl acted like she had better sense...."

"I heard what you said," interrupted Smith.

He spat tobacco and dragged his sleeve across his mouth. Then he chuckled.

"You'll have to get your dibs in quick. Every puncher with the herd's gonna be puttin' on the dog for her."

Chance started to reply, then let his breath escape without speaking. It was a waste of a man's time....

Chapter Twelve

After that they rode in silence while needlepoints of starlight began to poke holes in the umbrella of blackness above them. When at last they reached the rim of the mesa above the valley of the river, they could look down and see the embers of Solomon's cooking fire. The only sounds were the sounds of the bedded herd and the deliberate movements of the handful of punchers on night guard. A full moon was already starting its ascent.

"That your outfit?" asked Phike.

"That's it," replied Billy Joe.

Phike nodded toward the slope ahead.

"This looks like as good a place as any to get my wagon down off this rim."

Billy Joe motioned with his hand.

"Let's swing south a piece before we head down."

Will Phike jerked his hat brim down low over his eyes.

"Ain't nothin' wrong with right here," he said.

His tone left no room for bargaining. It was beginning to add up in Billy Joe's mind. Will Phike was a stubborn, unyielding man. He had a sudden feeling the two of them weren't likely to become fast friends.

But he made his voice level.

"We'd better move south a ways before we head down to the flats. If that bunch of longhorns yonder heard that wagon of yours comin' down the slope at 'em, they'd run from here to breakfast."

He waited, growing angrier by the second, while Phike studied about it.

At last the man on the wagon seat made up his mind.

"Well, I guess there ain't nothin' to do but follow yore lead."

With the moon's lanternlight showing the way, they circled south until they came to the slope Billy Joe was looking for, one gentle enough to allow the wagon to descend to the river level. He gauged the travel of the stars and judged it was past midnight.

Solomon wasn't happy about being prodded from his sleep, but then he learned the plight of the errant family. In minutes he had a fire blazing and beans and sowbelly and coffee growing hot on the coals.

The boy, Sidney, his sister, Charity, and Martha Phike ate greedily, with unembarrassed zeal. Will Phike tried to conceal his anticipation, but when Solomon handed him a tin plate heaped with cold biscuits and hot beans he could no longer contain himself. He attacked the plate ravenously.

Solomon stood beside the fire with a ladle in his hand and grinned a huge grin.

"By gadfrey, it shore does make a man feel good to see folks appreciate his cookin'. Now you take this bunch of uppity cowpokes. They ac' like they're too danged good to eat what I set in front of 'em ''

Every puncher not on night guard had crawled out of his bedroll when the squeal of the emigrant wagon had signaled its approach. They stood about now, with shirts hastily stuffed into trousers, as hungry for a look at the newcomers as those four were for a square meal.

T.Z. Riggs, who had seen his friend Alabama Pete snatched from his saddle by a Comanche bullet, finally asked the question they all wanted to ask.

"Didn't you folks see no Injuns between here and the Concho? I shore would have figured you'd-a run into a mess of 'em."

Will Phike kept eating, and it began to appear he didn't want to answer the question.

But at last he said, "We seen dust bein' kicked up two or three times. Hoped it was a wagon train or maybe a trail herd. But we never did get close enough to see."

Sidney spoke for the first time since he'd begun eating.

"Sis was afraid it was Injuns. So pa didn't signal 'em."

Billy Joe cast a quick glance toward Arlo Smith, who rolled his eyes in exaggerated comprehension. Then Chance said, "More than likely she was right. You crossed the plains right through Comanch' territory. Nobody with good sense would try to take a wagon train or a herd through that country."

He had been watching the girl and wasn't listening to what his own tongue was saying. The sudden silence jerked him up short.

Phike had stopped with a forkful of sowbelly halfway to his mouth. The girl was looking down at her plate. Behind his beard, Arlo Smith was trying to keep a grin hidden. At that moment, Billy Joe could happily have wrung his neck.

"Well, that's . . . What I mean is, that's not the usual trail across the Llano Estacado. Not for white folks, anyway."

He swore silently, gave Smith a go-to-hell look, and changed the subject.

"Either of you womenfolk know anything about patchin' up bullet wounds?" he asked. "We've got a man with a bullet in his chest."

The girl looked up. The firelight glinted brightly in her eyes.

"I might be of some help," she said.

Chance nodded and pulled his gaze away, toward Will Phike. He had no hint of the reception his next words would receive.

"You're welcome to throw in with us as far as Fort Sumner, Mr. Phike. There are no guarantees, but you'd be better off travelin' with a herd than going it alone."

Phike stood up. He was a lean man, stooped a bit at the shoulders, but even then he was tall, every inch as tall as Billy Joe.

"I'm obliged," he said. "But there's no reason why we cain't make it now. We'll just foller the river. Oughtn' to have any trouble."

Billy Joe took the cigarette from his mouth and threw it into the fire.

"How you ever made it across the Llano without losing your hair, I'll never know. But you're sure pushin' your luck, Phike."

He waved a hand to the north and east.

"That's Comanche country. They say the Plains Indians have all been rounded up and moved to a reservation. But you'd have a hard time convincing those half-dozen punchers we've buried of it."

He waved his left hand in an arc that took in the world to the north and west.

"And that," he said, "is Apache country. One or the other will have your hide before you get a day up the trail if you insist on travelin' alone."

"I thank you kindly but we'll go it by ourselves," said Will Phike. And then he added, "I don't intend to be beholden to nobody."

Charity brushed back a stray lock of reddish brown hair from her face. Her tone was quiet, matter-of-fact.

"Pa, maybe we ought to listen to Mr. Chance."

Phike frowned.

"I said we'd go it alone, girl. I've made up my mind."

Meekly she nodded assent, but then she said, "We can talk about it in the morning."

Phike was angry. He opened his mouth to speak but Billy Joe interrupted.

"And that's not very far off. We're pulling out at first light."

A puncher took down the lantern hanging at the rear of the chuck wagon and fell into step beside the girl as she moved toward the canvas-topped wagon.

"Let me help you folks get settled," he said.

Chance had started to turn away. He looked back. It was Whitey with the lantern.

Arlo Smith trailed him as he led his horse to the rope corral that held the remuda.

"Now ain't that somethin'," said Smith. "Ol' Whitey ain't never done nothin' for nobody. Not until now. He's already sniffing 'round that little gal like . . ."

"Shut your face, Smith," Billy Joe snapped. "I don't give a hoot what Whitey does as long as he does his job with the herd."

"Course you don't," replied Arlo Smith, nodding briskly. "Any fool kin see that."

But they didn't get started at daylight as Billy Joe had planned. One of Will Phike's oxen was down and refused to get up. Seeing the team in the full light of morning, Chance wondered how the beasts had brought the wagon as far as they had. They were drawn and gaunt.

"There ain't no more meat on them critters than on a pair of starving jackrabbits," said Arlo Smith.

Phike bristled.

"There's nothin' wrong with these animals," he said. "We'll be hitched up in a bit."

He took a long, woven rawhide whip from his wagon

and swung it whistling across the back of the brindle ox that refused to stand. Still the animal lay without moving.

Phike cursed and lashed at the ox with his whip but it was of no avail. The ox had gone as far as he would go.

Billy Joe signaled to Smith.

"Cut out a likely looking steer from the herd," he said.

"What are you thinkin' on doin'?" demanded Phike.

"Gettin' you hitched up so we can get this outfit moving," said Chance.

"You go on and let us be," said Will Phike.

Billy Joe ignored him and watched as Smith and another drover led a mottle-faced, red roan steer to the wagon. Whatever it was they had in mind for him to do, the big steer wasn't eager to find out. He balked at sight of the wagon and braced his legs against the ground. Smith took a dally around his saddlehorn and dragged the roan steer into place.

Stretched out with a rope around his horns and one around his hind legs, the steer was yoked beside the brindle ox.

"It ain't gonna work," said Phike. "He'll tear my wagon to pieces."

"Yeah. You're probably right," said Billy Joe, and then he shouted at Solomon.

"Get some grease over here and grease this off wheel."

That done, he motioned for Phike to take a seat on the wagon.

"He's all yours," he said.

The girl stood beside his horse and looked up at him.

"What about the other one? We can't just leave him here."

The sun was high, the herd was moving, and Billy Joe felt his patience wearing thin.

He drew his Colt and offered it, butt first, to the slender girl.

"Shoot him," he said.

She jerked back her hand.

"How could you? . . . I'll not shoot him. He saved our

lives." She drew a deep breath. "Why don't you shoot Mr. Stroop? He's holding you back too, isn't he?"

Billy Joe holstered his gun, feeling foolish.

"Your ox will be all right. He's got water and plenty of grass. He'll survive."

She shook her head.

"The Indians. They'll kill him."

"Naw," he said. "They don't like beef. They'd rather have horsemeat. Now, if you don't mind, let's get on with it."

Once more they started north. To Billy Joe it seemed that a long, slow year had dragged by since he'd first set eyes on this herd and had words with Whitey and talked Gideon Stroop into taking him on. But it had been little more than a month. And the distance they'd traveled was not yet as great as the distance that lay ahead.

Watching the longhorns move out in a ragged, uneven line of march, he wondered whatever had possessed him to accept Gideon Stroop's offer as straw boss. Probably because Whitey was so dead set against it, he decided.

Well, he and the ex-straw boss would have a lot of settling up to do when the right time came. Whitey would see to that. He'd already given notice.

Chance frowned. Whitey had something sticking in his craw, something more than the fight they'd had at the campfire. And something that went even further than the demotion from straw boss to trail hand.

He shrugged. That was sometime in the future. There were plenty of problems to occupy a man's mind right now. He sat the dun horse on the rim of the mesa and watched Will Phike's attempts to coax the mottle-faced roan steer into pulling his share of the wagon's hitch.

Even from that distance, Billy Joe could hear the rifle-shot explosions from the tip of the rawhide whip as it bit patches of hair from the longhorn's rump. From time to time he could hear Phike's voice, but the span of the cap rock was too great for him to make out the words.

"Strange gent," Billy Joe murmured aloud to the dun horse. "Been out in the sun too long, I guess."

Chapter Thirteen

He hesitated when he knew he shouldn't have, hoping for a glimpse of the half-spindly girl who had all the frailty of rawhide. But she didn't come into sight and he suddenly spurred the dun gelding into a fast lope toward the point of the herd, where a trail boss was supposed to be.

It was four days later that Billy Joe found the opportunity to know Charity Phike better. He wished the opportunity had never come his way.

She had asked to ride in the chuck wagon, where she might see how her wounded patient, Gideon Stroop, was faring against the heat and the painful jolting. It was a reasonable enough request. And Chance had already seen that Charity Phike wasn't one to take her responsibilities lightly.

Solomon's wagon was in the lead and Will Phike's dilapidated rig was far to the rear. The herd, at Chance's direction, was moving north along the mesa two or three miles from the ragged bank of the Pecos. The longhorns made better time there, even though they had to be pointed down to the river to water at the end of the day.

Billy Joe was riding Stroop's blue roan horse that morning. He swung the roan away from the point of the herd and eased down off the slope of the mesa toward the river. He wanted another look at the level of the current, a level that had already dropped measurably in the short span of time they'd been following the river's course.

Idly, he noted the tracks where the chuck wagon had passed, read the sign in them where Solomon had stopped briefly, and wondered for a brief instant why the cook had halted the wagon. Then he rode on through the ragged, shoulder-high brush to the water's edge.

His first impulse when he saw the unexpected, flesh-colored movement in the water was to draw his Colt. He knew it wouldn't be one of the trail crew, not while the herd was moving. And no Indian on earth would be caught dead in skin that color, skin with the paleness of fresh cream. Then his horse broke through the last fringe of brush and he sat looking at the naked back of Charity Phike, standing to her hips in an eddy of the Pecos River current.

She heard the sound of the horse and turned instinctively, a sudden look of fear on her face. The flicker of relief that replaced the apprehension was short-lived. She caught up the muslin washcloth and held it before her, and then she understood from the look on the trail boss's face that the tiny piece of cloth was woefully inadequate for the task demanded of it.

She dropped to her knees, leaving only her head and shoulders protruding above the swirling surface of the water.

"You . . . How dare you!" she gasped.

Billy Joe felt his face turning hotly crimson and he wanted to swear.

"Ah, well . . ." he mumbled, shifting his eyes from the girl's face to the deep blue of the Guadalupe Mountains swelling upward along the western horizon.

She was regaining her senses.

"What are you doing here?" Her voice rose shrilly. "Why aren't you with the cattle?"

"I thought you were in Solomon's wagon," said Chance.

"I was. I was," she said. "But then he stopped and let me out so I could bathe before our wagon gets here. Solomon said no one would come."

Billy Joe was angry at the girl for his embarrassment, and angry at himself for what had gone through his mind during those first moments of shock.

The blue roan was trying to get himself a drink and his forelegs had bogged to the knees in the soft soil along the bank of the stream. Billy Joe reined him about with such force that the horse reared precariously for a moment before regaining his footing.

He rode through the curtain of brush that screened him from the river and Charity Phike, and said without looking back, "Your pa's wagon is coming."

"Just . . . just go on," she shouted.

But the admonition wasn't necessary. Billy Joe Chance had the roan horse in a dead run, away from the river and toward the spearpoint of longhorns up on the mesa. The wind failed to cool his flushed, crimson face.

It was a savage country through which they were trailing now. Billy Joe marveled that any white man had had the courage and the iron will to forge a trail across such a raw, unfriendly land. They had long since left Texas and the bit of white man's civilization is represented. Now they were in a part of the world that knew no civilized law except the force a man could bring to bear with his own wits and strength, or with the gun in his hand.

Paralleling the Pecos River on the east was a continuing escarpment of sandstone cliffs, broken only occasionally by ravines that split the line of bluffs and provided a means to reach the higher tableland that bordered the river.

Westward—a direction to which Billy Joe's gaze was drawn with increasing frequency—were the sharp, rugged spurs of the Guadalupe Mountains, the land of the Apache Indians. Although driven from the plains by the Comanche horse warriors, the Apaches were still a threat to herds following the Goodnight-Loving trail to Fort Sumner.

Led by such chiefs of cunning and courage as Cochise, Victorio, and the fox-witted subchief named Geronimo, the Apaches continued to defend their mountain strongholds against assaults by the United States Cavalry and depradations by the Mexican army. But it was only hearsay to Billy Joe Chance. He'd never explored this deeply into the savage vastness of the West, although he had been often in the company of men who had. And to those men he had paid close heed.

Now, the nearness of the ominous range of mountains made his throat go dry. He had already lost too many men to Comanche bullets. If a war party of Apaches chose to attack, his crew would be hard pressed to stand them off.

In addition to that, the herd had already been thinned by more than a hundred head as a result of the stampede touched off by the Comanches, and twenty-odd horses were missing from the remuda for the same reason.

Billy Joe looked along the 150 miles of uncertain trail that led to Fort Sumner and pulled his hat down tighter.

"Yeah," he said to the horse beneath him, "I sure was smart taking on this outfit."

Indians and stampedes weren't the only hazards he had to watch for. There was the ex-straw boss, Whitey, who'd rather see Chance fail as trail boss than ride a new saddle. The whole lot would be better off if Whitey and his sidekick, Mule Hunnicutt, were given the sack right now, but every hand was needed.

He glanced back and saw the white overjet of Will Phike's wagon moving at a snail's pace beyond the drag. Of the dumb moves he'd made since taking on the trail boss's job, that probably took the prize as the dumbest. He should have let Will Phike dig his own grave. But then Martha and Sidney and the freckle-shouldered girl named Charity would have shared that grave.

Suddenly he heard a thunder of hooves and turned to see Arlo Smith riding hell-bent for the ridge where he was sitting the roan.

"Chance, ain't you seen 'em?" shouted the old cowboy when he was still fifty yards away.

"Seen what?"

"Them redskins, dang it. Look over yonder."

The gray, straggling beard on Smith's chin was shoved forward like the wattles on a turkey gobbler's neck. He pointed northwestward, toward a ragged series of breaks in the mesa above the Pecos.

They were not hard to see. A half-dozen horsemen were moving their way at a long trot. And beyond the small band of riders was a larger gathering of Indians, some afoot and some on horseback.

"To hell with the herd. I'll get the boys back to the wagons and head for the breaks. We'll have a chance to stand 'em off there," Smith said, wheeling his horse about.

"Hold on," ordered Billy Joe.

"What do you mean, hold on?" snapped Arlo Smith. "We're fixin' to have ourselves a war with them Injuns and you wanna hold on?"

Chance pointed toward the contingent of horsemen moving toward them.

"Look again," he said.

Smith squinted toward the approaching riders, extending his neck forward as though to shorten the distance.

"Well, they ain't the same bunch that made a run at us before. But they're Injuns, all the same."

Billy Joe pointed again.

"One of em's carrying a white rag. Stuck up in the air on the barrel of his rifle."

Arlo Smith spat a long stream of brown past the shoulder of his horse.

"Yeah, I believe that. Just like I believe a rattlesnake rattles to say howdy. I'm gonna gather some of the boys up here whether you like it or not."

They came on, the band of mounted, dark-skinned warriors. One carried a lance, another a bow and quiver of arrows, but most had rifles.

Billy Joe didn't look around but he heard the drovers moving up and spreading out in a thin line along the ridge. The longhorns would have to look after themselves for a time. This bunch of drovers was ready to fight.

"It looks like they want to powwow," said Chance.

He looked around and saw that every cowboy had his carbine out of the boot and lying across the swell of his saddle. To one side, away from the rest of them, was Whitey. He had dismounted and was hunkered down behind a broken-off outcropping of sandstone. His .50 caliber Spencer rested across the bench of stone in front of him.

"I don't want any shooting unless they make the first move," said Chance.

He jerked a thumb over his shoulder. "Tell 'em that," he said to Arlo Smith.

Smith was back in seconds.

"Them ain't Comanches," he said.

"No. Apaches, more than likely," Billy Joe said. "They're not looking for a fight. At least, not right now."

"Well, I trust 'em about as much as I would a one-eyed longhorn cow with a day-old calf," muttered Smith. "I don't like the smell of it, and neither does this old pony."

The six Indians rode up the ridge toward the line of drovers, totaling more than twice their number. That alone took a measure of nerve, Chance mused.

The warrior in the lead had a piece of dirty white muslin tied to the barrel of his rifle. It was a repeating rifle, Billy Joe observed, the only one among the weapons carried by the braves. The others with rifles carried old guns, single-shot actions, for the most part.

They rode straight on, looking neither left nor right, but moving directly toward Chance. When they were two horse lengths away, they stopped. For a long minute, the Indians surveyed the line of Texas cowboys, and the drovers stared back. They'd never had an opportunity to study a bunch of Indians, live ones, at close range.

Chance held up his hand, palm outward. The Apache warrior with the flag of truce dipped his head, almost imperceptibly, causing his long, straight black hair to stir slightly. His eyes never wavered from Billy Joe's face.

"Are you the chief of this trail herd?" he asked.

Billy Joe was startled. Except for a slight Spanish accent, the Apache's language was almost flawless.

"That's right," said Chance.

"My name is Shohanno," said the brave.

He nodded to the horseman on his left, a broad-faced warrior with a flattened nose.

"In your tongue he is called Breaks His Nose. He is my segundo."

Chance felt the tension draining from him. He had been ready for anything.

"Mine's Chance," he said. "What can I do for ya?"

Shohanno gestured with the rifle, drawing a semicircle in the air toward the north.

"This is our land," he said. "Your cattle are crossing the land of the Apache."

Billy Joe nodded, his face emotionless.

"I understand," he said. "But we will be gone from here in a few days, no more."

"You are driving to the Bosque Redondo?" It was a statement more than a question.

Billy Joe nodded.

Once more Shohanno waved his hand in an arc, gathering in the world from the Guadalupe Mountains to the distant beginnings of the Pecos River.

"All of this is Apache land," he said.

"There's some of them Comanches that don't know that yet, I reckon," drawled Arlo Smith.

It was the wrong thing to say. The Indian stiffened perceptibly. He spoke briefly in Apache to the warrior on his left, the one he had called Breaks His Nose. The tone of the meeting had taken on a sudden chill.

Billy Joe shot a quick glance of rebuke at the old cowboy.

"Well, it's the damned truth," said Smith.

"Just keep your trap shut and let me do the palaverin'," snapped Chance.

He turned back to the Apache warrior.

"I understand the words you speak, chief," he said. Nodding toward the Indians visible in the distance, he asked, "How many are there in your band?"

Shohanno had no intention of divulging that number.

"We are a great many," he said.

Twice Billy Joe held up both of his hands, fingers extended.

"Twenty would hit it pretty close."

Shohanno's expression gave no sign that the leader of the cowboys had come within two of guessing the correct number.

"We are many," he repeated.

Chance nodded.

"Five," he said. "I will give you five steers to feed your band in exchange for crossing Apache land."

Five longhorns would be a small enough price to pay. But there was no answering nod from Shohanno. For a moment, he and Breaks His Nose spoke in the tonal, indistinguishable tongue of the Mescalero Apaches.

"No," said the Indian leader. "We do not want your cattle. It is horses we need."

"Horses!" exploded Arlo Smith.

"Shut up," said Chance. To the Indian he asked, "How many?"

"Fifteen."

Billy Joe looked long into the expressionless eyes of the Apache leader.

"We have no horses to spare. We have already lost many head to the Comanches."

For no longer than the flicker of a hawk's shadow passing overhead, he read in Shohanno's gaze something more than inscrutable silence. It was gone in an instant but it had revealed much.

"It is horses you must pay to follow the trail to the Bosque," the Indian said.

"What happened to your horses, chief?" asked Chance.

"That is of no concern to you." The Apache pointed with his nose toward the remuda out on the mesa, moving north at a distance from the herd. "You have many extra horses. Fifteen is the cost you must pay."

Billy Joe smiled a half-smile.

"Did the Comanches steal some of the Apache horses, too?"

It was as though he had physically struck the leader of the Apache band. For an instant, Shohanno's broad, dark face lost its impenetrable mask and Billy Joe knew his deduction had struck home. It was no secret that the Comanches and Apaches were eternal enemies. And that, on horseback, the Comanches were the superior warriors.

But it was a very sore point with this Indian and Chance wished he hadn't said it.

"Your tongue is loose," said Shohanno. "What is your answer?"

"I cannot let you have the horses," said Billy Joe. "I will give you instead ten steers. That's more than fair."

Again, the two Apaches conversed briefly. It seemed to Billy Joe that the second-in-command, the broken-nosed warrior, might have been arguing for acceptance of the ten steers. But Shohanno's word was law in that band of braves, and he would settle for nothing less than the horses.

Glancing toward the distant collection of Indians who had remained behind while their chief came to parley, Chance knew his guess had been correct. The Comanches, probably the same band that had attacked the trail herd, had also struck among these Apaches. That, no doubt, accounted for the missing horses.

At that moment, Billy Joe regretted that his experience with Indians was limited to the Plains tribes, Comanches and Kiowas, mostly. He didn't know how to get inside the mind of an Apache.

At last he said, "What do you say? Do you want the steers?"

Shohanno looked across the prairie toward the rest of his band. They were a great distance from their home in the high, rugged reaches of the Rocky Mountains and some were going to have to make the journey on foot. It had not been a good hunting excursion for his people.

Abruptly, Shohanno extended his left arm above his head, closed his fist and jerked it downward, and pulled his horse's head about. The powwow was ended.

Billy Joe watched the half-dozen braves ride away, their heads high and their backs as straight as the shaft of a lance. All six could have been shot from their horses, and they knew it. But not a one gave a backward glance.

Arlo Smith slid his hat off and drew his shirtsleeve across his damp forehead.

"What do ya think?" he asked.

Chance kept his eyes on the departing riders, whose pace was still deliberate and unhurried.

"I don't think we made 'em particularly happy," he said.

"What do ya suppose they'll do now?"

"My guess is we've seen the last of 'em. They've lost all they can afford to lose, to the Comanches. They'll be headin' on home."

Shohanno and his lieutenant, Breaks His Nose, and the other four braves were halfway to the band that had stayed behind. They moved up a rocky slope and for a long instant were skylighted there. That's when the shot sounded.

Chapter Fourteen

The explosion of the rifle was totally unexpected. Chance's horse sprang sideways. He jerked it about and saw the smoke still issuing from the barrel of Whitey's Spencer. Quickly he turned back and was in time to see the Indian on the spotted horse throw his hands into the air and tumble from his pony.

With an incredibly long shot, Whitey had put a bullet between the shoulder blades of the Apache called Breaks His Nose.

Billy Joe spurred the roan into motion. He heard Mule Hunnicutt shout, "That, by damn, was some shot, Whitey." And Whitey, getting to his feet behind the outcropping of sandstone, smiled broadly.

"Now," he said, "they've got theirselves an extra hoss. That Injun won't be needin' his no more."

Chance drew up, dismounted, and strode toward the ex-straw boss. Whitey was still smiling when Billy Joe hit him full in the mouth. Whitey's knees gave and he fell backward against the slab of stone. He struggled to his feet and Chance hit him again, putting all his anger into the driving force of his fist.

A ragged seam opened along Whitey's cheek and blood oozed down the paleness of his jaw. Once more he started to get to his feet and Billy Joe swung again, his knuckles colliding with Whitey's forehead. It was a poor choice of targets and Chance felt the shock of the blow all the way to his shoulder. Pain shot through his forearm.

But Whitey didn't want any more. He sat down abruptly, sinking weakly back against the stone. The old Spencer rifle lay in the red earth.

"I oughta put a bullet through your thick skull," said Chance.

"Yeah, well, maybe you'd better do it while you can," answered Whitey, through puffed lips. "Them's only Injuns."

The knuckles of his hand still smarting, Billy Joe mounted and rode away. He didn't look back although he knew what was in Whitey's mind. A bullet through Chance's back, like the one that had dropped the Indian, would go a long way toward salving the sting of the blows he had taken.

In the distance, the Apaches had picked up the fallen warrior, laid him across the back of his spotted horse, and rode on toward the main party. Billy Joe cursed under his breath. Shooting an Indian who was shooting at you was one thing. Pulling the trigger on one who had come to parley under a flag of peace was something else again.

He had a feeling they'd live to regret Whitey's moment of rashness.

Arlo Smith trotted up.

"Ain't no need of me askin' what you think of Whitey's little game. I seen what you did to him. And I enjoyed every bit of it."

Chance rubbed the knuckles of his right hand.

"Yeah, but it won't pacify those Apaches, I'm afraid. Did you get a look at where they went?"

"Disappeared off yonder, toward the river," said Smith. "They're not in any shape to fight much, I'd say. Not with half of 'em afoot."

"Well," said Billy Joe, "we can't wait around to see what they do. We've got a herd of longhorns to move. Seems like we spend a hell of a lot more time shootin' at Indians or stoppin' stampedes than we do trailing steers."

Arlo Smith pulled his hat down and loped away

toward the bunched-up drovers, who were still talking about Whitey's long-range shot and the interesting few minutes that followed. But they didn't wait for Smith's arrival. They knew what had to be done. In seconds they were scattering out to tighten up the herd and get it pointed north again.

It was the middle of the afternoon when Billy Joe first noticed the change. Westward, as though the rugged Guadalupe Mountains were giving birth to them, a bank of clouds began to build. Almost while he watched, they grew to a broad, thick canopy that blotted out the sun. Billy Joe sniffed at the air and smelled the sharp, pungent scent that lay heavy in the stillness. Nature was girding her loins.

He rode back and fell in beside Arlo Smith at the swing of the herd.

"All hell's gonna break loose from the looks of that cloud bank," he said. "Let's turn 'em down to the river and bed down as quick as we can."

Arlo Smith pushed back his hat and squinted in the direction of the swollen, pregnant mass of clouds.

"Aw, I don't know, Billy Joe. I've seen it cloud up like that every day for a week and never turn loose enough rain to put out a cigarette."

"Well," said Chance, "I'd as soon not risk another run. We've lost about all the time and steers we can afford to lose."

Arlo Smith shrugged.

"Whatever you say, Mr. Trail Boss."

He turned and rode ahead toward the point.

Thunder muttered restlessly along the distant horizon and the herd was nervous. The steers didn't want to graze, nor did they show much interest in bedding down. At last, though, they began to settle in, all but the fish-belly steer. He kept up his ceaseless watch around the perimeter of the herd.

Solomon was midway through fixing the evening meal when the first drops of rain started to hit. They were huge drops, each one as fat and broad as a silver dollar.

Solomon ordered the erection of a sheet of canvas over his preparations.

Will Phike drew his wagon to a halt not far away and he and his family hurried to the scant protection of the canvas canopy as the rain began to fall in earnest. Billy Joe watched Charity take the wrap from her head and shake out her hair, hair about the color of a light bay horse, he decided. And he'd always had a liking for bays.

Unexpectedly he remembered the picture she had made standing in pink innocence in the shallows of the Pecos earlier that day.

At that moment, she looked his way and he felt the heat rise in his face, and swore under his breath. A trail herd had no business taking on the burdens of a wagonload of pilgrims who couldn't find their way out of sight.

Chance took his plate and moved in against the wagon where the rain touched only lightly. He was surprised when Charity Phike came and found a place no more than the span of a wagon wheel from where he stood.

They stood that way for three or four minutes, neither saying anything. Then she spoke.

"Do you think those Indians will come back?"

He shrugged.

"I don't know," he said. "What would you do if some idiot shot your best friend in the back?"

She was quiet for a time. Her next words were unexpected.

"I guess I owe you an apology, Mr. Chance." Her face, dotted with tiny beads of moisture, was a bright crimson in the glow of the campfire.

He knew what she meant, but he said, "How's that?"

"Down at the river. This morning. I should have known better."

Billy Joe frowned at the food in the tin plate in his hand.

"Well," he said gruffly, "It's dangerous to wander off by yourself in this country."

"I'm used to taking care of myself," she said matter-of-factly.

He looked down at her face and saw that her full lips pulled up at the corners easily, as though at some time in the past she might have smiled a lot. He noticed again the sprinkling of freckles across her small nose. There had been a scattering of freckles on her shoulders, he remembered. And a few in other places.

A cold drop of rain rolled under his shirt collar and down his back. That, he supposed, accounted for the goosebumps along his spine.

Arlo Smith came up then. Water was running from the brim of his hat and spilling onto the ground and his slicker was bright with rain.

"On second thought," he said to Chance, "you might be right. Maybe it is gonna rain a mite."

He took off his hat and wiped the moisture from his face with a wet sleeve.

"If it ain't too much bother for you to think on right now, Mr. Trail Boss," he said with too-casual indifference, "how do you feel about doublin' up the night guard? Them ol' steers still ain't settled down like they ought to."

Billy Joe's answer was sharper than he intended.

"You're straw bossin' the outfit, Smith. Just go on and see to it. You don't need me to hold your hand."

Arlo Smith went away muttering to himself.

"He's a nice old man," said Charity Phike.

She didn't put it into words but her tone carried a hint of reproof. Everybody, it seemed, wanted to tell him how to run his affairs.

"Uh-huh," he replied. "But he runs off at the mouth a lot."

She sipped at her coffee while he ate. He was strangely ill at ease in her presence. He hadn't spent much time in the company of young ladies. That time in Abilene, at the end of a drive, was about all. But he'd been doing some celebrating then. And that lady was no lady.

The silence dragged on until, out of self-consciousness, he had to make conversation.

"Your pa. What's he planning to do in Santa Fe?"

She turned her gaze to Will Phike, standing at the very edge of the canvas sheet that turned the rain. There

were too many people under the canopy, so Will Phike was
making sure he didn't get in the way. He was half in and
half out of the canopy's shelter, and the rain fell on the old
yellow slicker around his shoulders.

"He wants to go into business there," said his daughter. "If he can borrow the money."

Chance thought about it for a time.

"Your pa's pretty much his own man, I'd say."

She looked at him.

"What do you mean?"

"He strikes me as an independent sort. Not much for
letting other folks tell him what to do."

"Yes," she said. "That's right. No one tells pa what
to do."

She hadn't said it in so many words, but she had
included herself in that description. Billy Joe studied her
face again and decided that what he'd thought was warmth
and friendliness in the set of her mouth was more likely
longheadedness.

But then she added, "I just want you to know, Mr.
Chance. I appreciate your letting us travel with your herd.
I don't know if we'd have made it. . . ."

The words trailed off.

"No trouble," he murmured. "Glad to be of help."

She looked in the direction of the longhorns, bedded
down reluctantly in the chill rain a hundred yards' distance
from the wagons.

"You don't really expect them to stampede, do you?"

Chance shook his head, droplets of rain breaking free
in a tiny shower from his hat brim.

"A man can't really tell about those critters. They
might, and again they might not." He paused, remembering
previous occasions. "It doesn't take much to set 'em off.
In this kind of weather, especially."

She stood silently beside him for several minutes. The
uneasiness he had felt at her nearness had diminished. He
was on the point of deciding that he didn't mind Charity
Phike standing close enough to touch. *Hell*, he thought. *I
don't know what I think.*

Then he looked toward the fire and saw the silhouette

of a bull-necked man with heavy shoulders looking their way. Whitey had been watching throughout their conversation.

"You'll excuse me, ma'am," said Billy Joe, touching his hat brim. "I'd best see to things."

"I was going to tell you how Mr. Stroop is getting along. . . ."

Chance went past the fire and dropped his plate in the steaming wash pot. Whitey, his eyes following, leaned toward Mule Hunnicutt and spoke a word. Mule grinned a broad grin that failed to improve the ugly of his face.

Billy Joe shrugged into his slicker, irritated for a reason that wasn't clear. He cursed at the rain running down his neck and wished he still had the carefree outlook of a cowhand instead of the burdens of a trail boss. It was amazing how quick a man could collect a peck of trouble simply by standing in one place too long.

He swung into his wet saddle and eased out toward the herd. Arlo Smith was there, making sure the double guard was in position.

"Get finished with your socializin', did you?" Arlo Smith inquired with innocence.

"No," snapped Chance. "I didn't. But I figured someone with more sense than a pissant ought to see how these steers are taking it."

"The man lookin' after these steers knows a heap more about what he's doin' than some others I can name," said Smith. "And so far he ain't fell in love with any of 'em."

He rode on into the wet blackness. For a moment, Billy Joe thought he heard the old man humming a tune to himself.

The herd was uneasily quiet, the steers stoically withstanding the sting of the rain in their faces. After a time, Chance rode back toward the chuck wagon. Arlo Smith fell in beside him. Nothing more was said about Charity Phike.

"So far so good," said Smith. "I believe we're gonna make it till daylight."

Billy Joe was watching the western horizon, pure black except for brief instances of erupting brilliance.

"Maybe," he replied.

He went on strapping the rawhide hobbles about the black's forelegs. He hadn't mentioned it to his straw boss but he wasn't satisfied with the bed ground on which he'd put the longhorns. Because the weather had cooled, he had settled them on a slope. But that had put them a shade too close to the wagons. It wasn't a comforting thought.

Still in wet clothes, Chance crawled into his bedroll beneath the chuck wagon. The rain hadn't relented any to speak of. It wasn't sluicing down in sheets like it had been, though. Now it was a steady drizzle, the kind that could find its way through tarps and wagon beds and, after enough time, even forty-dollar John B. Stetsons.

After a couple of hours of fitful dozing, Billy Joe propped himself up on an elbow and looked into the darkness. The drizzle continued unabated and the wind was kicking up, whipping the rain beneath the wagon bed. He muttered a disgruntled oath and pulled on his wet boots. A man was wasting his time trying to sleep in weather like this.

In the saddle once more, he rode the black horse gently and carefully back to the herd's perimeter. The lightning that had trifled in frivolous flickers along the horizon had become bolder now. Bolts of brilliance shot across the sky from the rafters of heaven to the floor of the prairie, showing him the sodden earth and the bedded steers and the riders hunched here and there in their saddles.

Ivy Spurlin came riding from the night, repeating the words of a plantation melody in a sort of singsong chant.

"How do they look?" asked Chance.

"Well, Mr. Chance," replied Spurlin. "They're about as calm as a weanlin' pig caught under a gate. I ain't took a breath for the last half-hour for fear of settin' 'em off."

Lightning tore a great, jagged rent in the blackness of the atmosphere and a peal of thunder drowned out his last words.

"A couple more hours and we'll be in good shape," said Billy Joe.

Chapter Fifteen

At that instant another bolt of blue-orange fire speared downward from the heavens, bathing the prairie with an eerie brilliance. They both saw it at the same time. A short distance from the wagons, in the relentless drizzle, something moved. It was a man, a man on foot, with a slicker thrown about his shoulders. The wind caught the yellow garment and billowed it upward, revealing for the barest instant a pair of legs, long, skeletal, and unclad.

Behind him, Billy Joe heard a steer blow a frightened blast of air from his lungs. The fish-belly longhorn had also seen the strange specter.

"Aw, hell," breathed Chance.

The sight of the man on foot was the last straw. The lead steer bawled a sudden complaint and was gone into the darkness. Instantly, twenty-eight hundred of his brothers were on their feet in frenzied pursuit.

"Get the boys!" Billy Joe shouted to Spurlin, and then he sent the black horse into the even blacker tunnel of night after the frightened cattle.

The steers bolted north, for a time paralleling the Pecos River on one side and the upsweep of ragged breaks on the other. But then they found a slope and poured up the cap rock to the plain above. Billy Joe could hear their labored breathing and the rattle of clashing horns. From time to time another bolt of lightning turned the black of night to midday and he could see the rippling current of steers boiling across the prairie like bits of debris swept along by a raging river current.

He had the feeling he had lived this moment before.

Without reason, the stampeding steers turned abruptly to the left, back toward the river. Chance felt them

crowding toward him and he knew there was no chance to
wheel them into a mill away from the breaks. On they
came, and he turned the black pony away, fleeing the
crazed torrent. Salvaging his own life suddenly became of
pressing concern.

The steers swept on by him and shortly were upon the
lip of the cap rock. Mindlessly, they poured over the rim
and down the sharp slope. Some went over the edge where
there was no slope, only a straight wall that ended in a
tumble of rocks below. They bawled plaintively when their
feet left solid footing and the realization came that they
were hurtling to destruction.

Chance reined the hard-breathing black to a halt at the
edge of the abyss. There was no turning this stampede
now. He could only hope no drovers had been caught in
the run.

As though ashamed of the catastrophe it had kindled,
the storm suddenly subsided. The rain ceased as quickly as
it had begun and the thunder and lightning retreated
eastward, rumbling in frustrated discontent.

With the coming of daylight, Billy Joe could see the
destruction. Scores of steers had plunged over the edge of
the precipice and were tangled in a mass of twitching,
broken backs and legs far below.

Out of the pale dimness of morning's first light rode
Arlo Smith. He sat his horse beside that of Billy Joe and
looked over the cliff. Then he spat an arc of tobacco that
shot outward and down toward the dead and crippled
cattle.

"Seems like our luck's holdin'," he muttered. "It's
as lousy as ever."

His glance touched Billy Joe's face, moved on, then
returned abruptly.

"You look mad enough to swaller a handful of
horseshoe nails," he grunted. "Hell, it wasn't nothin' but
a stampede. Ain't the first one you've seen."

"This time I know what set 'em to running. And I'm
gonna have me the hide of the man that started it,"
growled Chance.

"You wouldn't care to let me in on it, would you?" asked Smith.

Billy Joe looked back in the direction of the wagons. His face still mirrored his fury.

"As a matter of fact, I don't mind at all telling you. That old geezer, that Will Phike, was the one who touched the match to this particular explosion. And it's cost us another hundred head of steers, to say nothing of the two or three days it'll take to get the herd gathered in again."

He turned his horse about and spurred the tired animal into a fast lope back toward the wagons. Behind him in the infant light of day, Arlo Smith dragged a sleeve across the corner of his mouth, reined his mount around, and sent him along Chance's trail.

"Shore don't wanna miss this little prayer meetin'," he muttered to himself. "Oughta be more fun than a Saturday night in town."

The smoke from Solomon's cook fire lifted in a long rope toward the sky as the two riders started down the slope. The wrangler and his remuda were there but the other drovers were in their saddles and on their way up the river, already beginning the punishing task of collecting the herd.

Billy Joe rode straight for the Phike wagon, setting a short distance beyond the pair of trail wagons. Arlo Smith followed close behind.

"Phike!" Chance's voice slashed through the morning silence like the shattering of a looking glass.

There was no response from within the canvas-shrouded wagon.

"Will Phike," he called again. "Come out here."

There was a stirring at the tailgate of the wagon, and in a moment the angular form of Will Phike descended to the ground. He was in boots and pants but without a shirt. A patch of curly gray hair ran the length of his narrow chest from chin to belt buckle.

Will Phike was not intimidated. He shrugged into his shirt and looked up at the angry man on the horse.

"I'll thank you to keep your tone civil," he said. "Now, what is it you want?"

"I'll tell you what it is." Chance's voice rang hard and clear in the dawn like a blacksmith's hammer smiting an anvil. He was unaware that Charity had emerged at the front of the wagon and was listening to the exchange. "It was you that set those longhorns to running, Phike. What in hell would any sane man be doing galavantin' around in the middle of the night in a storm like that?"

Will Phike's drawn, thin face turned a deep crimson, but there was no hint of apology in his voice.

"If you're talkin' about last night in the rain, I sure did get out of my wagon. I got out to answer a call of nature. They ain't no law ag'in that, I guess."

Billy Joe's glance found Charity standing by a front wheel of the wagon, but he was too full of anger to care.

"It was a damn fool thing to do, Phike. You out running around on foot with a slicker waving in the air. What did you think those steers would do? They're probably still running. The ones that didn't go over the cap rock and break their necks."

In contrast to his tone, Charity's voice was soft and unemotional.

"You can't blame pa, Mr. Chance. Anything could have caused the stampede. You said yourself the cattle were likely to run."

Billy Joe wasn't in any mood to listen to the reason of what she was saying.

"Beggin' your pardon, miss, but you keep out of this. It's between your pa and me."

Will Phike saw his chance to hit back.

"You won't talk to a member of my family like that, Chance. I won't stand for it."

Billy Joe's wrath swept him on, past the point where his better judgment cautioned him to stop.

"I'll talk anyway I take a notion, Phike. I'm the man that's got to answer for what happens to this outfit." He drew a deep breath. "I should have left you out there with the buzzards and coyotes instead of letting you come along with the herd. I've had nothing but trouble on my hands since. . . ."

He looked into the stricken face of Charity Phike and

realized he had said too much. She turned away, but the light of the new day had touched a tear glistening among the freckles on her cheek.

"Aw, forget it," Billy Joe said with disgust. He pulled the black away.

But the honor of Will Phike had been pricked to the quick. No man would talk to him like that.

"No," he said sharply. "I'll not forget it, Mr. Chance. You're right. I shouldn't have throwed in with your outfit. We was making it just fine without yore help."

He turned toward the wagon.

"Martha!" he barked, the word as sharp-edged as an oath. "Get out here."

Instantly, it seemed, Martha was climbing down from the back of the wagon. She had obviously dressed in a hurry. Her graying hair was tousled and her long dress was askew on her plump body.

"Martha," said Will Phike, "you go get our things from the chuck wagon. We're pulling out."

"Yes, Will," she replied meekly, and she scurried away toward the wagon of Solomon.

Billy Joe was in a tight. His anger was spent now, but there was no recalling the words he had said. He had no great love for Will Phike, but, like an oriole building its nest bit by bit, the man's daughter had fashioned a permanent niche for herself somewhere deep within his being.

"I'm not asking you to leave, Phike," he said at last. "I'm just telling you how it is. What you did was a fool thing to do. You've cost us a hundred head of steers and two days, maybe three, of getting 'em gathered again. It's done and over."

Will Phike stepped back to his wagon, rummaged in a box near the tailgate for a moment, and withdrew a piece of paper. Without comment, he began writing.

Chance looked back over his shoulder. Arlo Smith sat astride his cow pony a few paces away. The old cowboy looked at Billy Joe, rolled his eyes toward the glowing pink of the fresh, new sky, and aimed a stream of tobacco downwind.

Phike strode the few steps to Billy Joe's horse.

"This here's an IOU for the steer you give me," he said, reaching up. "I'll redeem it when I get set up in business in Santa Fe. You don't need to fret that it won't be paid."

Billy Joe frowned and shook his head.

"Hell, Phike. The damage is already done. Just let it drop."

"I ain't about to let it drop," said Phike, indignation growing in his voice. "We'll be movin' on so's you won't be bothered with us no more. Now, if you'll excuse me, I'll get to hitchin' up."

Charity was still standing by the front wheel. Chance's gaze touched her for an instant. She looked away, biting her lower lip.

Feeling like he'd lost a war, Billy Joe rode away with Arlo Smith at his side.

After a time, he said angrily, "Dammit, the old man shouldn't have been out in the rain flapping that blamed slicker. Any fool oughta know better."

"Yeah, that's right, Billy Joe. You did right runnin' him off and lettin' him and the womenfolk and the kid find their own way through the badlands and the Injuns and the Comancheros with that piece of junk he calls a wagon."

Chance jerked his gaze toward Smith.

"Just what the devil you tryin' to say?"

"Me? I ain't tryin' to tell you nothin'. It ain't your lookout if them pilgrims get their hair lifted by the 'Paches. Fer instance, that bunch that got one of their braves blowed out of his saddle by yore friend Whitey."

Billy Joe didn't feel like listening to Arlo Smith explain in detail what might happen to the lone-traveling wagon of Will and Martha Phike and the boy Sidney. And the freckle-faced girl named Charity.

"Shut up," he snapped. "Just shut the hell up."

"All I said was . . ."

"I heard what you said. Now get to gatherin' them steers before they get plumb back to Texas."

It was a time of restless brooding for Billy Joe Chance. He changed horses, rode to the bluffs overlooking the river, then pulled up and turned around. On the flat below, he saw Will Phike's wagon jerk into motion. It moved up beside the other two wagons, and he saw a figure walk quickly to the hoodlum wagon.

That would be Charity Phike, Chance knew, refusing to leave until she had taken a final look at the wounded man she had volunteered to care for. A few moments later, she returned to her father's wagon and it moved away, cutting a pair of slow, muddy tracks northward, away from the trail wagons and the campfire.

There rose in Chance's breast another impulse to ride down and tell Phike once more what kind of fool he was for leaving the protection of the herd and striking out on his own. But then he remembered the bitter, resentful look in those squinted gray eyes that morning. There would be no changing that old man's mind.

He turned his horse and rode away across the mesa in a long lope, trying to shut out the picture of the hurt in the face of the girl while he and Phike were exchanging angry words. She understood the danger. She didn't want to go. And that, of course, was the only reason for her reluctance. It had nothing to do with the fact that she was riding forever out of the life of a green trail boss who didn't know when to keep his mouth shut.

Ah, if only he had that few minutes to live over.

The main herd had swung in a wide arc across the sodden prairie and then back to the cap rock bordering the river, but the tracks showed plainly that here and there along the course of the stampede, bunches of steers afflicted with the same madness had splintered off and gone their own way, for reasons that only a longhorn could understand. There would be no quick regrouping of this trail herd.

He drove the men hard and himself even harder. Along in the afternoon of the second day, Arlo Smith caught up with Chance as he whipped a handful of gaunted steers back into the main bunch along the river.

"Maybe we ought to ease off a bit, Billy Joe," said Smith. "No point in runnin' 'em until they drop in their tracks."

Billy Joe's face was grim.

"I want this herd back together before dark today. It's already cost us two days we don't have to spare."

Arlo Smith took off his old hat and dragged a sleeve across his forehead, where a few strands of gray hair were plastered by perspiration.

"I heard somebody say once that Rome wasn't built in a day. I wasn't sure what that gent was tryin' to say, but I have a suspicion he was talkin' to a trail boss with a cockleburr caught under his tail."

He sent a glance toward the sun hanging hot and bald and heavy in the sky above the ominous raggedness of the Guadalupe Mountains.

"What I think is, I'm talkin' to another trail boss that's mad at himself because he run off a wagonload of greenhorns and now he's worried they're liable to land in trouble up to their armpits in the middle of a bunch of mad Injuns."

He cocked an eye at Billy Joe.

"How close would you say I come to callin' it about right?"

But Billy Joe wasn't ready to admit it.

"Quit worrying about me and get to worryin' about gettin' this herd back into one piece. That's what a straw boss is supposed to do."

Arlo Smith jerked down his hat, spat a stream of tobacco toward the westering sun, and grunted. "Yore memory ain't too good. You just shoved the job at me. I ain't never agreed to take it."

He reined about to ride away.

"Worst mistake we ever made was lettin' that bunch of pilgrims ride along with us for a few days. He's got that little freckle-faced gal stuck in his craw and it looks like the rest of us are gonna have to suffer through a bad case of puppy love."

Billy Joe jerked around.

"What'd you say?"

"I said there ain't no way we can get this bunch of longhorns back together before sundown. Anybody with a lick of sense can see that."

Arlo Smith was right. When the sun rose the following day, Chance saw the count was still short, even after figuring in the several score that had been killed plunging from the bluff in the wild blackness of the stampede.

He called Smith to his side.

"I'm gonna make another swing and see if I can pick up any tracks. We're still short two, maybe three, dozen head. Much as I hate to, we'd better hold the herd here until tomorrow."

He started away, then stopped.

"I'd best look in on Stroop."

Arlo Smith pulled at one big ear and shook his head.

"He's still out of his head, Billy Joe. Fever's eatin' on him pretty bad."

"Yeah, I know," said Chance.

At the hoodlum wagon, he turned back the canvas cover and peered inside. Solomon was there, taking off the dirty old cloth that covered the wound and replacing it with one only slightly less dingy.

"Any change?"

"Cain't tell it if there is," said Solomon. "I'm still managin' to get a little gruel down him now and then. He ain't woke up enough to say anything."

With a fresh horse under him, Billy Joe rode up the slope to the rim of the cap rock and turned to look at the outfit spread along the river below. The chuck wagon and the hoodlum rig looked somehow incomplete without Phike's ancient schooner bogged in the sand nearby.

Downriver, beyond the wagons, was the trail-toughened remuda, searching out what graze they could find on the flat that bordered the river. Three-quarters of a mile upstream, the main body of the herd was grazing unconcernedly, as though there had never been the thought of a stampede in their obstinate, longhorned heads.

It all looked serene, peaceful. Chance started to swing the lineback dun horse away and push his search for the handful of errant steers that had managed to elude the riders. Even in the act of reining the dun about he felt a nagging worry. There was something wrong with that panorama of wagons, horses, and cattle below him. It was too calm, too tranquil.

Back down the slope he rode and sought out Arlo Smith, catching himself another horse from Julio's remuda.

"I thought you was gonna make a quick swing around the rest of the world and find them other steers," said Smith, pulling the latigo tight on an ugly, Roman-nosed mustang that watched from the corner of a treacherous eye for an opportunity to take a bite of cowboy.

"I'm fixing to," replied Chance. "But things look a mite too peaceable to suit me. You keep your eyes peeled, savvy?"

Smith drove a fist against the mustang's nose and stepped into the saddle.

"Well, Mr. Chance," he said. "Since this is my first day on the job, I surely do appreciate the advice from an old hand like yoreself."

He started to spit, remembered he hadn't yet bitten off a chew of tobacco, and reached into his pocket. The sarcasm faded from his voice.

"What's eatin' at you, Billy Joe?" he demanded. "Everything's goin' slick as butter. We'll be in Fort Sumner in another three weeks, soon's we get out of this mudhole and get the herd movin'."

Chance was scanning the horizon to the west and the north and not listening to the old man.

"Tell you what. Split that remuda. Leave half of 'em here and send Julio up on the cap rock with the other half. Take 'em a couple of miles away from the river and hold 'em there."

Arlo Smith grunted but it was not a sound of agreement.

"That don't make no sense at all," he said.

"Well, take care of it anyhow. Hear?"

Chance rode away, back up the long incline to the lip of the mesa above the river. Arlo Smith spurred the mustang in absentminded irritation, then spent the next three minutes turning the fresh air a sulphuric blue while the tough little horse did his best to unload him into the buffalo grass.

Billy Joe had an idea where the twenty or thirty head of missing longhorns might be. A deep arroyo, flecked with greasewood and thick patches of mesquite, cut a ragged gash across the bald prairie a few miles from the river. It was a likely covert for longhorns raised in the thickets of south Texas.

He reached the shallow beginnings of the arroyo, dropped off into the ravine, and saw immediately that his suspicions had been correct. The tracks of a dozen and more longhorns led into the dense underbrush. He heard sudden hoofbeats behind him and grunted with satisfaction. He'd need whatever help he could get to pry these outlaws loose from their hideout.

He turned in the saddle and saw a horse coming fast, but he couldn't see the man in the saddle. Well, it didn't make any real difference, as long as it was a Texas cowboy rather than some redskin scalp hunter.

Suddenly, the other rider burst into view. Billy Joe jerked the dun to a sliding halt. The puncher coming through the thicket at him was Whitey!

Without reason, he was suddenly irritated. Any other member of the crew would have been welcome. But not this one. Whitey had followed him for a reason.

The ex-straw boss pulled the stout bay down a few yards from Billy Joe's own horse. For a long moment Billy Joe sat his heaving cow pony and studied the other man. It wasn't likely he'd come along for the fresh air.

"What're you doing here?" He kept his voice even, without malice.

But the question was unnecessary. What Whitey was doing there showed in his face. It was an angry, crimson face, pinched around the mouth.

"I come to have a little talk with you, Chance," said the ex-straw boss.

"You could have done that back at the herd. That's where you're supposed to be, anyhow."

"This here's private. Just between you and me."

Billy Joe felt his own anger growing.

"I told you we'd settle it when we got the herd to Fort Sumner. Now I suggest you hightail it on back to the herd."

Deliberately, Whitey drew a sack of tobacco from his shirt pocket and began to roll a smoke. He completed the cigarette, slipped one end between his lips, and fired a match on his saddlehorn.

"I've had about all of you I can stomach, Chance," he said, eyeing Billy Joe through the smoke of the cigarette. "What do you say we settle our differences right here, where there ain't likely to be nobody to bother us?"

For an instant, Chance was tempted. Whatever was eating on Whitey, it didn't seem to be getting any better, and his bitterness was a constant source of discontent for the other drovers. Win, lose, or draw, a showdown right here would eliminate one nagging worry.

But a trail boss couldn't afford that luxury.

"Sorry, Whitey," he said. "You'll have to wait till we get to the Bosque. We've got a herd to move."

Whitey's face was flushed now and puffy with bottled-up anger.

"I'd say your problem is, you ain't got no backbone, Chance." He paused to draw a deep breath. "Maybe it runs in the family."

Billy Joe stiffened.

"You've got something stuck in your craw, Whitey. You've had it for a long time. Now spit it out."

Whitey's voice had the prickly sound of a Russian thistle whispering in a winter's wind.

"O'Bannon!" The name burst from his lips. "That name mean anything to you?"

"I recollect hearing it," said Billy Joe. "What about it?"

"Then you recollect a couple of boys named Calvin and Newt O'Bannon, maybe?"

It was suddenly falling into place for Chance.

"What about 'em?"

"Them boys were cousins of mine. Them two you gunned down back in Tennessee." His gun hand was low, resting casually against his thigh. "O'Bannon's my name."

Later, Billy Joe realized it wasn't as much of a surprise as he would have figured. Maybe it was the albino look of Whitey, the same look he had seen in others of the Tennessee O'Bannons. Or maybe it was simply that he knew he'd sooner or later run into another member of the tribe and have it to face again.

But the chill was still there along his backbone. Abruptly, he saw it all again: the mules straining against the wagon's traces in the Tennessee mud, his pa's slow, steady voice giving them encouragement, and the sudden appearance of a dozen riders, bursting around them under the rain-soaked umbrella of red oak trees.

His sixteen-year-old heart had climbed into his throat and choked all the air from his lungs. And later, when Newt and Calvin had gone away and left his pa standing on that three-legged milking stool with a rope around his neck, he had wanted to cry but he couldn't because that wasn't a Chance's way.

Now, looking into the face of Whitey and knowing he was an O'Bannon, Billy Joe had to fight down a sickening surge of hate. He wanted to forget his promise to his pa and plant a bullet somewhere in the bushy white brows between those pale, emotionless eyes.

"Were you there that day? When they got pa and Tom Roy?"

Billy Joe had trouble saying the words and he could see that Whitey knew it.

"That's right. I was in the bunch amongst the trees when they stopped your pa's wagon." He grinned with one corner of his mouth. "You was a scared rabbit, you was."

The painful memories and the old fears were receding. Chance's voice turned hard.

"Then you rode with the rest of 'em when they went to get Tom Roy?"

"Yeah. I rode with 'em. They made me stand lookout, though. Said I wasn't old enough."

He said it regretfully, and Billy Joe knew it was the truth he was speaking.

"How'd he die?"

"He fought like a damned wildcat, until they put enough lead in him to where he couldn't pull a trigger no more."

Billy Joe was remembering what he had seen there at

the shack when he had pulled up with the body of Ruben Chance in the back of the wagon.

Whitey pushed back his hat, letting a thatch of colorless hair fall across his eyes.

"You're the last one left, Billy Joe Chance," he said. "And I still owe you for Newt and Calvin."

Chapter Sixteen

The pure pleasure of hammering back his six-gun and blowing out the lights of another O'Bannon leaped into Billy Joe's throat. He didn't realize until that moment how much he had wanted to do it over the years.

But he had made the promise to his pa that there would be an end to the feud, and nothing had happened to change that promise. He sat his horse and looked into the eyes of the other man and swallowed back his hunger for the smell of burning powder.

He shook his head.

"Whitey, if you were anybody else in the world, you'd be stretched out there on the ground turning stiff. The fact that you're an O'Bannon is the reason you're not."

A quick frown of puzzlement touched the other man's face. But he said, "The reason that ain't happened is because the sun hasn't risen on the day a Chance could take an O'Bannon in a fair fight—fists, guns, or what have you."

His breath was coming quicker.

"We'll do it a-settin' on these horses, or we'll step down and pace it off. Just whichever way you want it."

There wasn't going to be any way out of it. Chance could see that in the hard, pale eyes of the other cowboy. There was going to be more spilling of blood in the Chance-O'Bannon feud in spite of his vow to his pa.

He found suddenly that he didn't want that. Whitey was a worthless bully, with all the merciful instincts of a prairie rattler. But he had been no more than a kid, just as Billy Joe had been, when the other members of the O'Bannon family had hanged Ruben Chance and shot Tom Roy to death. A shootout with Whitey O'Bannon because of that long-past feud would serve no end, except to violate his promise to his pa. And hadn't his pa's spirit already suffered enough?

While these thoughts went through his head, Whitey watched his face with burning intensity. Whitey wasn't afraid of the showdown, and it suddenly occurred to Chance that he might very well have met his match with this cowboy. For the first time in a long time, Billy Joe had a momentary doubt about his own quickness with a six-gun.

Then Whitey snorted, "Hell!"

He threw his reins to the ground and stepped down from his saddle.

"Get off your horse, Chance," he commanded. "One of us is gonna be laying here lookin' at a buzzard pick out our eyes in another half-minute. There ain't gonna be no more fancy little tricks like you done before. There ain't gonna be no more puttin' off this here particular judgment day."

Billy Joe sat the stocking-legged sorrel horse and looked down at the man on the ground. He could read in Whitey's eyes what the man was thinking. O'Bannon knew, as well as did Billy Joe, that a man standing with two feet planted firmly on solid earth had a decided edge over a man on horseback when it came to speed in pulling a gun or accuracy in shooting.

And now Whitey owned that edge. It was simply a matter of time before his rage reached a level sufficient to push him over the brink.

Chance's mouth was suddenly dry. He had felt he could control what happened here, between him and Whitey, but now he wasn't at all sure.

His gaze traveled in a sweep around the horizon and

then it dropped to Whitey's drawn-down mouth. It was
time. It was Whitey's time, at least.

He was watching Whitey's eyes and wondering if it
was going to end here when the gaze with which he had
touched the horizon sent a signal to his brain. Knowing
O'Bannon was at the knife edge of shooting him, he
almost put it out of his mind. But it rang too loudly.

"Now, Chance, you lily-livered pup," shouted Whitey,
and he dropped into the smooth, quick crouch of a man
who had more than a nodding acquaintance with a six-gun.

Holding the reins in his left hand, Billy Joe threw his
right hand into the air, and came as close as he had ever
come to taking a .45 slug in his chest.

"Hold it!" he shouted, and pointed with the upraised
hand.

It was almost more than Whitey could do to stop the
pulling of the trigger. But there was a deep urgency in
Chance's voice that snapped his head around.

"Yonder," said Billy Joe, still aiming his index
finger.

Slimly, dimly on the horizon northwest of where the
two cowboys had talked about death, a rope of black
smoke crawled skyward until it reached a thousand feet,
then broke over and drifted away toward the Rocky Mountains on the skyline.

Whitey wasted only an instant on the ribbon of smoke
in the rolling, treeless tableland, then he turned back.

"You lookin' to weasel out? That don't signify nothin'."

"That's got the smell of Apaches," snapped Billy
Joe. "I've got business there. You do what you want to
with that six-shooter in your hand."

He knew it was a risk. He felt the prickle along his
spine, like a centipede squirming upward between his
shoulder blades.

But he didn't look back. He spurred the sorrel into a
run toward the distant stroke of ragged black painted
against the blue of the sky. He forgot the stampeded steers
that he'd set out to find, and he forgot the face of Whitey
O'Bannon with the hunger for killing rooted as deeply in

his being as the taproot of a mesquite tree growing at the edge of a dry arroyo.

It was a handful of hot sand that lay in his mouth and spilled down his throat so that he couldn't swallow. That strip of black smoke was a dozen miles, maybe fifteen, north along the Pecos from the point where the herd was being regathered. The distance—and this time he couldn't stop the dry swallowing—was about the distance the wagon of Will Phike would have traveled after leaving the trail-drive camp early the previous morning.

Anger and pride had driven the old man and his family away from the safety of the herd. How much of the blame for that should be his, Billy Joe wasn't ready to think about.

A half-hour later he pulled the heaving sorrel horse to a sliding stop on the cap rock above the river and looked down the rocky slope. The sight that met his eyes twisted at his gut. The signs were all there, as easy to read as a wanted poster. Will Phike's old wagon had burned to a skeleton, but it was still smoldering. There was no sign of life, or of death, from where Billy Joe sat, but he had no doubt of what he would find.

Then he rode down the slope.

The old high-wheeled wagon that had held all the dreams and hopes of the Phike family would never move again. The household goods it had held were scattered in a ragged circle on the ground about it. Things like drawers from a chest and a handful of cooking utensils and an old shoe were thrown aside. Whatever bolts of muslin or other cloth that might have been in the wagon were gone, along with the rations Chance had insisted that Solomon provide the Phikes before they pulled out.

Billy Joe rode around to the other side of the burned hulk. Will Phike was the first he found. The old man had had no time to dress. He wore only his trousers, with one gallus jerked across his shoulder, and his socks. He had held up both hands to ward off the bullets of the Mescalero Apaches. One of those bullets had penetrated his hand and his throat and he had fallen forward onto the sand, spread-eagled, with blood soaking in an ever-darkening circle around him.

They had made no effort to take his scalp, Billy Joe saw. It wasn't much to look at, anyway; a few scraggly gray hairs that would not enhance even the most beggarly lodgepole. He recollected, too, that the mountain Apaches weren't long on taking scalps. That was a practice they had learned from the Mexicans. Now, they occasionally took one for celebration purposes, perhaps, but even then the warrior who took it was not permitted to join the victory festivities.

Billy Joe felt a quick surge of tangled emotions as he looked down at the mortal remains of Will Phike. It had been predictable; he had told the old man what he faced, trying to go it alone to Fort Sumner through country that Apaches claimed as their birthright. And those Apaches had an extra reason for hating those of the pale skin, after Whitey O'Bannon had, for no reason except cruel idiocy, shot the Mescalero warrior from his horse.

The Apaches must have taken a great deal of pleasure in laying waste to this lone wagon and its helpless white-eyed occupants.

Billy Joe looked over his shoulder for Whitey, not wanting to hurry his inspection of the carnage lying there in the sand. Where was Martha Phike? Where was Sidney, the magpie-chattering kid with the snaggleteeth?

And Charity Phike? The girl with the freckles, and the quick, sensitive mouth and the piercing eyes that could spot a man's weaknesses from fifty yards in poor light? Chance didn't much want to know the answer to those questions, and he was somehow glad when he looked up and saw Whitey's horse top the ridge.

The flies were busy about their work when Whitey drew rein beside the wagon. He looked down at Will Phike's body while Billy Joe studied his face. There was a different kind of paleness there, for a moment, a gray-ash look that added years to his age. Whitey didn't want to look at the old man's corpse.

Silently, Billy Joe gigged his horse in an ever-widening circle, knowing that putting it off wouldn't help. Twenty yards from the wagon, in the sand-rooted shoots of rushes along the riverbank, he found Sidney. The boy had not died without a fight. But the impatient Apache hadn't wasted an arrow or a bullet on an insignificant kid. The warrior had merely snatched up the boy by the heels, swung his head against the metal-rimmed hub of a wagon wheel, and tossed the body into the weeds.

But evidence of Sidney's resistance was there. He had managed to get his teeth into the arm of the Mescalero brave. There was still a shred of Indian-brown skin caught between his teeth.

Billy Joe turned away. The two oxen, the bobtailed one and the animal Billy Joe had ordered cut from the herd and hooked to the wagon, were both lying dead, the puncture wounds from numerous Indian lances marked by blackened rivulets of blood across their necks and down their chests.

Anxiety spread through Billy Joe like the first, deep rattling chill of influenza. Charity Phike and her mother were all that remained. What would the Apaches have done with them? Taken them for their own slaves? Or simply used them and dumped their bodies in the red-sand tomb of the Pecos?

Billy Joe found the tracks of a few horses leading away from the wagon, toward the river's edge. There were only a few pony tracks, followed by a number of bare, broad footprints. Chance studied them closely, attempting to pick out the one or two that would be those of Charity and Martha Phike.

Then he jerked his head up. The party of mounted Apaches that had visited the trail drive in hopes of trading for additional ponies had possessed more horses than this. Where were the others?

Whitey was still on his horse, wandering through the scattered remnants of household goods. He had made no move toward burying the bodies of Will and Sidney Phike, or much of anything else.

"They're gonna hit the herd!"

It was all Billy Joe had time to shout before he bogged the sorrel around in the red sand and spurred him south. Whitey understood immediately. In an instant, his gray horse was charging after Chance's mount. They had a ride of a dozen miles to the gathering ground. Shohanno and his angry Mescalero Apache warriors would be far ahead of them.

Chance's fears were confirmed in the first quarter-mile. He saw the tracks of Indian ponies, stretched out in a dead run over the rugged cliffs that bordered the river's course.

Billy Joe knew they were too late. He'd ridden a wide circle beginning in the early hours to get a lead on the missing steers, then Whitey had ridden up and they'd had their little confrontation that had come within a gnat's whisker of erupting into flying lead.

Then there was the ride to the point on the river where the wagon of the Phikes was smoldering. And now they were still a frightful distance from the herd and Solomon's campground and Gideon Stroop's sickbed in the hoodlum wagon. The Apaches would have had total surprise on their side.

Chance turned to look at Whitey's face. That was the man who had, in all likelihood, set this whole deadly chain into motion by shooting an Apache brave from his saddle just to impress a few of his cronies. Without that single moment of stupidity, the Apaches might have ridden back to their mountain stronghold.

It was a greater distance—an endless distance, it seemed—back to the herd. The stocking-legged sorrel was starting to stumble and Whitey on his gray horse was back behind somewhere, not even in sight. Then Chance saw the first wisps of smoke drifting skyward on the still air from down in the river flat and he knew his prophecy was correct. The Apaches had split their force, giving the old men and the squaws and the kids the job of eradicating the helpless wagon of pilgrims upstream while Shohanno and his mounted warriors had headed south toward the herd. They would not be going back to their lodges empty-handed, even if they had to lose a brave or two in exchange.

Suddenly, there it was below him, spread out for a

half-mile along the Pecos River flats. It was worse than the massacre of the Phikes simply because of numbers. Burning wagon hulks and bodies sprawled on the ground and slain horses and a few dark-skinned Indians made the scene look like an unrealistic painting Billy Joe had seen once of something called "Custer's Last Stand." But this was real. Blood was still oozing from wounds, wounded horses were still thrashing, and the burning wagons were still sending up shaggy locks of black smoke.

He sat on his horse and pounded the saddle horn and cursed softly, without passion. He scanned the western skyline, thinking perhaps there might still be an Indian, just one maybe, who had hung behind to gloat. But there were none. They had vanished, blowing away like ghosts into the Guadalupe Canyons as soon as they had made their raid.

Billy Joe could see how it had been done. The Apaches, a dozen and a half, perhaps, had done the job. But it was the element of surprise that had given them the big edge. They were already in place about the chuck wagon and the sleeping cowhands and the sleepy night guard. They must have struck only a matter of minutes after Billy Joe had ridden away to cut for sign on the missing steers.

He swore again. It couldn't have been more than a half-hour. But the wind had been wrong and he and Whitey, that confounded Whitey, had heard no hint of trouble behind them as they rode up the cap rock and aimed northeast across the rolling prairie.

Billy Joe rode on down the sharp slope, skirting boulders and wicked clumps of thorny mesquite and scattered patches of salt cedar trees. His first view of death in that place was the body of a short, bow-legged Apache he recognized as one who had been among the half-dozen warriors who had ridden to the herd under a flag of truce to talk horse trade.

That sudden thought jerked Chance's head about. The remuda was gone! The horses he had left in the charge of Ivy Spurlin, to be held here on the flats, were gone. And Spurlin, the fat Negro who had graduated from a Georgia cottonfield to cowboyin', had paid the price of standing his ground.

Chance rode over. Spurlin lay on his side, curled into a ball against the attack he had known was coming. An Apache arrow protruded from his chest.

The other half of the remuda—the bunch he'd sent to the mesa under Julio's care. Had the Apaches found them, too?

But then out of the scrub growth along the river came Arlo Smith, leading his horse. There was a dirty strip of cloth tied about one arm, the gray fabric showing signs of fresh blood.

Chance hadn't realized how desperately he had wanted to see that ugly, grizzled face. Smith was a predictable element in a world turned suddenly upside down.

The old cowboy paused, looked Chance up and down a time or two, and growled, "You missed the party."

"How many got it?" asked Billy Joe shortly.

"I make it five. Those Injuns come at us from three sides, just after daylight. That Shohanno, that mean-lookin' booger that wanted to trade horses. He was leadin' 'em. And he danged sure wasn't carryin' no flag of truce."

He spat and let the residue run off his chin while he pointed.

"I guess they got old Ivy first. And two, maybe three, head of horses. Then they came in on us like a bad smell, settin' fire to everything and shootin' anything that moved."

"Who got it?"

Arlo Smith jerked his head toward the overturned hoodlum wagon.

"They got to Mr. Stroop pretty quick. He had got down so weak he couldn't have pulled a trigger if he'd wanted to."

Chance gigged his horse to the other side of the overturned wagon. Its contents were strewn about, fire still picking at the edges of a few bedrolls and odds and ends. Three paces away, in the red sand, lay the body of Gideon Stroop. He had been a big man when this trail drive began, back there when Billy Joe first saw him getting his anger

worked up enough to hang an old nester named Silas from
a cottonwood tree.

But now he was not so big. The wound from the
Comanche bullet had taken its toll, and the days of riding
in the wagon over clumps of salt grass had speeded the
gaunting process.

It had taken only one well-aimed Apache war ax to
put an end to Gideon Stroop's misery. Maybe it had been a
relief, Billy Joe mused.

"I found Riggs over yonder," said Smith at his
elbow. "He took a shot through the gut and then an
Apache lance through his neck for good measure."

Billy Joe wiped the back of his mouth with his hand.
It came away dry and sticky.

"How many more?"

"Three. Mule Hunnicutt was one of 'em. He was still
in his bedroll. And then a couple of 'em down along the
riverbank didn't make it." He spat angrily. "Damn them
Apaches for sneakin' coyotes, anyhow. They didn't open
up with their guns right away. It was arrows and lances to
start with. That's why we didn't get organized any quicker.
Them sidewinders are as slick as the dickens with them
arrows. Not like the Comanches."

"Well, they wanted horses, and they got 'em," Billy
Joe said.

"Not as many as you might suppose," said Smith.

"Half the remuda, I'd say."

"Not quite," said Smith, shifting his cud. "I got to
thinking about what you wanted to do with some of those
horses. Run 'em up on the mesa just in case. Well, I had
Julio take the whole remuda up there in that pocket. We've
still got the horses, except three or four, maybe. We just
don't have many cowpokes to ride 'em."

Then Arlo Smith's voice became acid. There was no
dry wit, no humor in it.

"Where's Whitey? I seen that wuthless scamp ride up
the cap rock after you'd been gone a little spell this
morning. What happened?"

"He wanted to introduce himself. His name is
O'Bannon. He's one of the family," said Chance.

"Well, I'm a son of a gun," exclaimed Arlo Smith. "An O'Bannon, huh? That explains why he's had such a mad on for you, Billy Joe. Guess he wants to keep the Chance-O'Bannon feud alive."

"Yeah, he was pretty anxious for a showdown," said Chance.

"Yeah, I'll just bet he was," snorted Arlo Smith. "I hope you left something for the buzzards to chew on."

Chance shook his head.

"We didn't get a chance to finish our business. There he comes now."

"What happened?"

"We spotted some smoke. Up north on the river."

"The Phikes?"

"Yeah."

"All of 'em?"

"We found only the old man and the boy. Both killed. I guess the women had been carried off."

"Damn!" exploded Smith. "That's the last we'll see of them pore womenfolk. They'd be a heap better off dead than bein' drug along by the Apaches. They'll make slaves out of 'em."

Billy Joe had already thought all those thoughts.

"Just be quiet about it."

Arlo Smith went on as though he hadn't heard.

"Some buck will have that little freckle-faced gal for a squaw. And the old woman. If she ain't handy at cookin' and stitchin' and such, they may hang her hide out to dry."

Billy Joe broke in.

"What about the herd?"

"They're still up around that bend yonder, in that brushy draw where you said to hold 'em. Them redskins weren't interested in driving a bunch of beef up into the hills no how. That's where the rest of the boys are. Up there with the steers."

"Solomon?"

"He dug hisself a hole in the creek bank and laid low. It'll take a heap smart Indian to sneak up on ol' Solomon."

Chance carefully fashioned himself a cigarette, concentrating on the damp, brown paper and the twisted crumbs of tobacco. He allowed his gaze to drift westward, across the Pecos River to the first rocky outcroppings of the Guadalupe Mountains.

"We've got to go after them," he said, half-aloud.

"Go after 'em? Go after who?" demanded Arlo Smith.

"The girl. The women."

"Have you lost the last little bit of sense you had, boy?" Smith almost shouted. "We ain't got a dozen men left and we've still got a herd to deliver. And you want to light out on the trail of those Apaches?"

He turned and sent a stream of brown into the red of the sand.

"Your cinch has done busted, boy."

"We'll see," said Chance. "Where's Julio?"

"If I know that Mex, he's halfway back to Fort Picket after hearing the shootin' that was goin' on here at daybreak," said Smith. "I hope he didn't turn the remuda loose."

Billy Joe waved toward the bluffs to the east.

"That's him now. And he's still got the horses. He's got more sand in his craw than you gave him credit for, Smitty."

Smith grunted.

"Yeah, he was probably afraid to run and afraid not to."

Chance watched the young Mexican wrangler come down the slope with the herd of horses and he breathed a sigh of relief when he saw the blood bay gelding, the one he'd taken from the Comanche warrior.

Whitey O'Bannon rode among the remnants of the burning wagons. When he stopped to look at the body of Gideon Stroop, his expression didn't change.

He eased his horse over where Chance and Arlo Smith were talking.

"Now what, big boss?" he inquired of Chance.

Billy Joe looked Whitey over, from his alkali-crusted black hat to his tied-down .45 Peacemaker Colt and on to his fancy spurs.

"You and me are going to have us a little ride after those Apaches," said Billy Joe calmly.

Whitey started to speak, swallowed at something, then started talking.

"You're out of your head, Chance. You're locoer than a Big Thicket steer. There ain't no way we can get them women back, and you know it. Two of us against two, three dozen?"

He shook his head.

"Forget it."

Whitey was tensed, ready to go ahead with what he'd tried to start earlier with his long-time feuding enemy. But the flashpoint didn't come.

"Whitey," said Billy Joe, "you shot that Indian from his horse yesterday while they were riding away. I figure you're a big part of the cause of this whole mess we're looking at right now."

He paused.

"We're gonna make a stab at getting those women back. If you don't have the backbone for it, say so."

Whitey's face went crimson.

"I'll take you on anytime, anyplace, Mr. Billy Joe Chance," he ground out through gritted teeth.

Calmly, steadily, Chance kept his eyes on the other man's face.

"What you're saying is, you don't have the stomach for takin' on some extra odds?"

Whitey didn't have an answer. His eyes dropped from Billy Joe's face, cut across Arlo Smith's frowning countenance with a bitter touch, and went on to the collection of horses that Julio was bringing up.

"I ain't crazy," he muttered.

Arlo Smith had been sitting silently on his horse, shifting from side to side in order not to miss any of the conversation.

Now he pushed back his dirty, high-crowned hat and, squinting one eye, looked at Whitey. But his words were for Billy Joe.

"Mr. Chance," he said, drawing out the word. "What I think we've got here is a hangfire. Whitey has made up his head he don't want anything to do with them Apaches. At close range, anyhow. So that leaves you and me. Now, what we can do, we can put one of the other boys in charge of the herd. Heck, Solomon could do it, for that matter. And then we can get to ridin'. Or we can kiss off them two women and get on about this infernal trail drive.''

Billy Joe looked at Arlo Smith and grinned.

''That's about what I had in mind. Except for one thing. Whitey here will be ramroddin' the outfit while we're gone.''

If he had leaned across and slapped O'Bannon with his gloved hand the albino cowboy's reaction would have been only a little less startled.

But Arlo Smith was the first to speak.

''You ain't leavin' that yahoo in charge, Billy Joe? Why, he's managed to mess up everything about this drive since we pulled out from the Concho. He's *pizen*, and you know it.''

''What do you say, Whitey?'' asked Billy Joe.

Whitey was looking around again, sort of as if he expected to see another cowboy sitting beside him. It was a half-embarrassed look he gave Chance.

''Why not.'' He shrugged.

''Aw, hell, Billy Joe,'' mumbled Arlo Smith.

Chance pointed to the rifle in his hand.

''Go get yourself some more shells. We'll have need of 'em.''

''I busted the firing pin on this piece of junk,'' said Smith.

''Well, grab the first one you can find while I saddle that catamount horse and let's get moving.''

Smith returned in minutes with a sack of grub and a long, double-barreled weapon.

''What the heck is that?'' demanded Chance.

''Solomon's ten-gauge. Couldn't find anything else.''

''That's not gonna be much good where we're going,'' said Chance.

''Well,'' drawled Arlo Smith. ''It ain't much on distance, but it's hell on scatter.''

Chapter Seventeen

Charity Phike stretched and felt a new ripeness across her abdomen and along her thighs. She hadn't yet become aware of the strangeness of the sounds coming from outside the wagon. There was nothing to hint that it was the spurting of blood from the slashed throat of an oxen that caused the minor disruption in the early morning stillness.

She looked around her in the grayness. Martha Phike and Sidney were still sound asleep, Martha's gentle snoring inside the canvas-topped wagon a paradox of peaceful tranquility in a savage wilderness.

At the far end of the wagon, Will Phike was sprawled loosely in sleep, but it was a fitful kind of sleep, in which his muscles jerked and his leg curled and straightened as though a bad dream were trying to jerk him upright into flight.

Charity had not often felt pity for her father. Rather, her relationship with him, since as far back in childhood as she could remember, had been one of gradually deepening hostility, of day-to-day animosity that she seemed unable to control. He wanted the best for his family and, when she grew into the early years of maturity, she wanted to lend him a hand, because she knew her mother was not cut from the type of fabric necessary to weather the great adventure to the West.

But the more Charity tried to help her father, it seemed, the more resentment built within him. He was the lord and master of the Phike family. Any suggestion by her that represented even a minor challenge to his authority was quickly cast aside, frequently with caustic, biting words.

"Girl," Will Phike would say in a tone that left no room for disagreement, "you're a woman. God meant for you to be a follower. That's why he put menfolk on this earth. To look after you and tell you what to do."

He would strike the table, or the wagon edge, or whatever was nearest at hand, and glare at her beneath his ragged, graying brows.

"Don't forget that. One of these day's you'll be lookin' to catch a husband. And there ain't no man worth his salt that would put up with the nonsense you're talkin'."

Often, in order to assure that she got the point, he would suddenly and without reason order Martha to fetch him his pipe or heat a kettle of water or stoke the fire. And Martha, round, soft Martha, would hasten to do his bidding.

On this morning of peacefulness in the wagon, she thought these thoughts about her father and found that her love for him was undiminished even though she knew deep within her being that it was as much her good sense as his that had allowed them to survive the crossing of the desert.

Then she became aware of the sounds from outside the wagon. The gurgling sound could have been from an eddy in the Pecos River current, but there was a heavy thumping, too, as might have been caused by a huge head beating against the sand.

Well, she reassured herself, they were a goodly distance from another soul. The trail herd was a day's travel behind them. And there was nothing to fear from the drovers. The trail boss, for all his young years, would see to that. For the duration of half a minute, she found herself comparing the two men, her father and Billy Joe Chance. Pulling on her sweater, she nodded absently to herself. Yes, there was something similar in the two men, something of an arrogant conceit that relegated women to a role, not of helpmate, but of indenture.

Half-angrily, she jerked on her shoes. These were useless thoughts, of value only to rankle and upset her. But as she put the thought away she knew that she, Charity Phike, possessed the will and the fortitude and the backbone to compete in whatever circumstances the world of men dictated.

The assurance lasted only a heartbeat. For she had looked again to where her father lay. A broad, brown hand was sliding beneath the canvas fly.

Charity screamed. At least, she thought that she did. But no sound broke the eerie quiet of slow-motion horror. The broad hand clutched suddenly about Will Phike's throat and he was jerked to an upright posture. In another instant, his angular body, kicking in wild, startled protest, was drawn from beneath the canvas cover.

Then Charity heard the booming sound of a gunshot. Slivers of oaken timber blew out inside the wagon. The big-bore rifle bullet had gone through Phike's body and had penetrated the oak sideboard.

She heard the quick, and final, intake of breath into her father's lungs, and the collapse of his body against the wagon, and knew that Will Phike had given his last command, had issued his last directive to plump, doughy Martha Phike.

After that, things happened too quickly to be placed in sensible sequence. At a half-dozen points around the wagon, the dirty, tattered fly was jerked up. Broad, expressionless Apache faces, nut-brown and framed by long, straight locks of raven hair, peered within.

Sidney awoke and screamed. Martha Phike, a flour coating of makeup on her face, a face flattened and broadened like a too-ripe cantaloupe, sat up suddenly, clutching the old coverlet about her upper body. Since tender years, no one had ever seen the actual flesh of her body below her neckline. Not even Will Phike, not for more than a glimpse, rest his soul.

Sidney fought against the hand that grabbed his sandy, unkempt hair and jerked him from the wagon. Charity saw him sink his teeth into the arm of the old, worn-out Apache brave and then she heard a cracking sound against the wagon hub, like a ripe pumpkin being dropped from shoulder height.

Then Charity heard the scream, and it was hers. This time she knew it was real. It began so deeply within her strained body that she had a momentary thought that she was going to relieve herself. The next instant, a pair of Apache squaws with wrinkled skin the texture of a horned toad's flanks were inside the wagon. One grasped the shoulder and ankle of Martha Phike and unceremoniously began wrestling her out onto the ground. The other took Charity's wrist and jerked her up. The touch of the rough hand and the pungent odor of the squaw's unwashed body left her weak and unresisting.

Charity had never been within smelling distance of an Indian. The odor and the impression were those of having been dropped suddenly into a cage of wild animals. Her mind simply refused to accept what she was seeing, except by bits and snatches.

She watched them pull her mother from the wagon bed. Poor Martha had never resisted anyone or anything in her life. She was doing her best to help them get her out of the oaken bed and onto the ground, but they never noticed.

Daylight had swooped down suddenly on that precipitous bend in the unpredictable Pecos where Will Phike had chosen to camp for the night. Charity could even hear a brace of crows cawing down from the dead limb of a cottonwood tree. She saw the carcasses of the two oxen lying sprawled in convulsive death kicks a short distance away and then jerked her eyes from that bile-triggering picture.

Her heart plummeted to the depths of her being. The number of Apaches was not so great; perhaps a dozen or fifteen in all. It was their unemotional stoicism that sent tremors of fright to the very soles of her feet. Were they human, or were they animals?

An aging Apache buck grabbed her shoulder and gave a sharp jerk, tearing her gingham dress to her shoulder blade. Then she was shoved into the foul-smelling embrace of a squat, unsmiling squaw.

Then they began their journey. There were three or four old men and a boy or two on horseback. The rest were women, squaws whose place it was to walk on the ground and build the campfires, and erect the tepees and gather roots and chew deerhide into soft garments. And to ensure that captives with white skin never for an instant forgot that they were of little value.

The crossing of the Pecos was treacherous. Once the twisting current jerked her from her feet and great torrents of stinging, bitter water filled her nose and throat. She coughed and retched and pulled back, but the powerful hand of the Apache squaw dragged her on, half off her feet.

Once she looked back, and then she didn't look back again. She remembered the tranquillity of the little campsite they had chosen the night before, and even some of the conversation around the driftwood fire after suppertime. They would reach Fort Sumner in a matter of weeks, said Will Phike in one of his rare, expansive moods. And then they would strike out for Las Vegas and then on to the territorial capital of Santa Fe, where the fertile soil of commerce beckoned.

He had made up his mind. This time, he told them, he would select an endeavor that could not fail. Transportation would be the thing. He would become a freighter.

The eyes of the other three members of the Phike family had touched each other briefly and then dropped. If there was something Will Phike was poorly equipped to handle, he doubtless had put his finger on it.

That had been last night. Only last night. It was all gone now. Will Phike would no longer purvey his instructions, directing his Martha to mundane, unnecessary tasks; or to shushing little Sidney, whether or not needed; or to spending uncertain admonitions on a daughter he didn't, and never would, understand.

Charity looked ahead and saw that two Apache squaws were struggling to lift her mother up the far, slick bank. It was almost comical. Martha Phike couldn't climb. Her legs had no strength. For every step she attempted she slid back another. At last, one of the fat squaws broke off a reed at the water's edge, jerked up the soaked, trailing dress that encompassed Martha Phike, and thrashed her sharply on the pink, round bareness of her legs. She scurried up the bank, then, and fell exhausted until the

Apache woman sent another stinging barrage of stripes against her legs.

It had been a long time since Charity had regarded her mother with more than casual indifference. Now she wanted to cry.

But abruptly her mind was jerked back to her own difficulty. The squaw who had been dragging her was thrust aside, and an old Apache warrior with wrinkled folds of brown skin hanging from his chest and belly grasped a handful of the full nest of hair on her head, hair that in the bright light of the sun gave off a strawberry-red hue.

She looked into his face and saw more than a solemn, inscrutable curtain. She saw for a bare instant that the fires of passion in this old Apache's belly had not turned to cold ashes.

Charity felt a faintness wash over her, and was afraid.

Then the walk began. The shoes she had pulled on hurriedly in the gray darkness were, in a dozen steps, it seemed, gone. Their captors led them up an arroyo westward from the river, toward the blue shoulders of the Guadalupes that vaulted upward in ragged ravines and vast, stone steps toward cold, distant peaks. Hostile high-desert plants jerked at her dress. The spears of lechuguilla blades and the fishhook barbs of rock-sprung catclaw tore the flesh from her lower limbs. She bit her lip, but the tears leaped anyway to her eyes.

It went on all that day. There was no noon stop to rest or to eat. The Apache women walked as though they could walk forever. Up sharp inclines, down steep trails to the little rush of water that trickled through the stones in the very bottom of the canyon. On each side, sharp slopes of rocky shale shot upward, slopes still covered with thickets and thorns and barbs that could maim and cripple.

Once, Charity looked up ahead, and then didn't make that mistake again. The world had grown vast and massive and overwhelming. Heavy, dark clouds clung to the peaks ahead. It would be cold at night at those elevations.

It was almost totally dark when the nighttime halt was called. Immediately, the squaws began to gather twigs for a fire, dry twigs with no green, smoke-emitting fibers to give away their position. Charity set about looking for tiny bits of wood to add. Her mother, though, was beyond movement. She collapsed in a shapeless heap against the ragged stone hillside, one hand to her heart. But the Apache squaw broke away the limb of a mesquite and whipped her legs soundly, so that the thorns cut great gashes and left trails of blood.

Charity lurched in between them, catching hold of the squaw's arms to stop the cruel beating. Effortlessly, the squaw cast Charity to the ground, and went on about her cold, methodical whipping of the bare, pink, bleeding legs of Martha Phike.

Charity didn't know what they were fed. Meat from some small rodent, dry as the sole of a shoe, that grew larger and larger as she chewed it. And a handful of dried, bitter mesquite beans. But the nourishment they provided was vastly greater even than the boiled tales of Joshua and Caleb, the oxen that had pulled Will Phike's old wagon across the Staked Plains to the gates of hell and left it burning there.

While they sat and ate and she listened to the unintelligible murmuring of the Apache tongue, Charity's eyes never left the face of the old Apache with the snakelike folds of dried, brown skin, the one the others called Stone Belly. She thought she knew what was in his thoughts and she was afraid. He pointedly ignored her and squatted on his haunches with the other old warriors, nodding solemnly at their sage observations, only once looking her way with the hint of a grin on his face. It was a hideous, toothless grin that caused chill-bumps to thrust out beneath her thin dress. She shrank farther into the shadows.

After a time, the Apaches rolled into their blankets and were instantly asleep. Charity and her mother, although not far from the old squaw who favored the mesquite switch, were neither bound nor surrounded. They were left simply lying together on the ground, to find warmth as best they could.

At first, Charity was astounded. The Apaches had taken no precautions to secure the prisoners. Charity and her mother could steal away in the night, back down the mountain trail toward freedom.

The thought was a fleeting one, short of life. She might, she just might, be able to get to her feet and stumble downhill for a mile, and try to hide in the bushes. But not Martha Phike. At morning she would be where she lay now, hopelessly and helplessly unable to move a muscle, to open an eyelid. If death came to Martha Phike during the night, she would embrace it eagerly.

It was the following day, a little before noon, when the old men and the squaws and their two captives were joined by Shohanno and his handful of raiders, those who had sped downriver to strike the trail herd.

Charity watched the riders come and held her breath. How had the attack gone? How many drovers had been killed? Was Billy Joe Chance among that number?

Shohanno was not happy. It showed in his scowling face and in the gruffness of his tone. He waved a short, disparaging hand at the pitiful number of extra mounts his warriors had added to their string of war horses. The chief had expected to return with many ponies from the trail herd. It had not been a good raid. There were still many of his band who had no horses to carry them to the remote fastness of their home in the high mountains.

Charity watched the eyes of Shohanno, the sharp ebony eyes of a hunting hawk, touch here and there among the small collection of old men, old squaws, and warriors-of-age. His eyes glided beyond her and then were jerked again to her face, as though drawn suddenly back by a rawhide thong.

He slid from his pony, tossed the single rein to a youth, and strode to the rock on which Charity sat. She couldn't look up at him. He reached out, grabbed her wrist, and pulled her to her feet. No, he actually snatched her into the air so that both her feet were dangling helplessly above the rocky ground. Then he threw her away from him, cast a contemptuous look at her scratched and bleeding limbs and her threadbare dress, and spun away. The movement was his expression of contempt for all the white eyes who had ever made war on the Apaches and raped their squaws and burned their tepees and taken their hunting grounds.

The girl looked at the hunting knife in Shohanno's belt and knew an instant of mortal terror. She would die here on this trail of catclaw brambles and her life would leak out and streak the stones with red-black necklaces of blood.

Shohanno stalked away, though, and Charity dared for an instant to gaze after his bronzed, sinewy back. And then her glance was drawn to one side, and she saw the face of old Stone Belly, his face and his eyes barely concealing his glee. She was his. She was Stone Belly's.

They pitched camp that night high up in a shallow, chiseled cave on a ragged mountain a wary distance from the little trickle of water in the canyon. Charity's mind was a cold numbness. She slept a fitful, terrorized sleep until a cold, silver moon oozed above the rim of the world's horizon, and then she smelled the scent of Stone Belly and his thick blanket, slick with filth, and felt the scaliness of his thigh against her flank.

It could not grow worse, she thought, but then the next day came and she understood that it could.

She first saw the Comancheros skylighted on their horses high up in the bluffs, and she wanted to shout and scream. These were not Indians. They wore big hats and boots and the clothes of men who were something other than savages.

The moment of thought that those riders on the skyline might be rescuers died a-borning in Charity's breast. There was a great deal of gesticulation and riding back and forth on the crest of the ridge by the five strange horsemen, but only the barest signs of acknowledgment among Shohanno and his band.

At last, the five seemed to gather their courage. Trailed by a pannier-laden mule, they reined their horses single-file down the steep mountain slope, sending before them a tiny avalanche of sharp-edged stones that came to rest in little mounds on the trail.

Martha Phike clung to Charity's arm as the riders drew to a halt.

"Who are they, Charity? Why do the Indians allow them to come? What do they want?"

Charity put a comforting hand on her mother's shoulder.

"Comancheros, I think they call them, mama. They trade with anyone. With Indians or whites or anyone."

Charity felt a tremor shake her mother's body.

"I'm afraid."

Charity looked down and patted Martha Phike's sunburned, peeling cheek.

"I wouldn't worry about them, mama. They'll go away when they've found something to trade for."

But Charity felt it too. A cold, gnawing fear in her belly. Even the Apaches had a certain savage predictability about them. But the five new riders had less the look of men than of wolves. Their leader was the one Charity couldn't pull her eyes from. He stepped down from his wiry, sweat-streaked little pony, and the sounds of his sharp-roweled spurs sang against the rocks along the trail.

He was neither tall nor short and his bowed legs were almost girlishly slender. But the roll of fat about his paunch was where one's eyes tended to linger. His belly was like the skin of a goat that had been sewn into a great pouch and filled with water, or with wine.

His mustache was long and black and well greased, and he touched it often, with affection. In his right hand was a plaited rawhide quirt, never at rest. With it he would strike the *chapaderos* on his legs from time to time to emphasize a point.

The name bestowed upon him at birth had long since been forgotten in a compendium of aliases. El Gallo—the Rooster—was what his followers called him.

Now, however, the Rooster gave no sign that he possessed the nature of a tyrant, nor that he viewed the Apaches with scarcely less contempt than he had for the lice that made their home at his scalp. But Gallo was no fool. He knew the temperament of the Mescalero Apaches, but more than that he possessed a high regard for the soundness of his own skin.

Reaching up with one hand, he slid his huge sombrero

forward from his head in the historic, servile *campesino* gesture of humility.

"*Hola*, chief," said Gallo expansively, smiling so broadly that the chancre sore at the corner of his mouth split and oozed blood. "We have come to make trade with the great Apache chief Shohanno."

Shohanno stood with his arms folded across his sinewy chest and gazed with indifference at the fat man in front of him. But Gallo was not deterred. He pushed his big hat onto the back of his head and dipped a hand deep into one of the *alforjas* lashed behind his saddle. From it he withdrew a roll of cloth and, with a quick movement of his hand, flipped the fabric outward. A long, yard-wide ribbon of satin-bright crimson, shot through with strands of silver, flashed sharply in the sunlight like a cutthroat trout leaping from a mountain stream.

It was an impressive sight there on the gray, rocky slope and Charity heard a young squaw catch her breath at the beauty of it.

Shohanno, however, gave no outward sign that he was moved by Gallo's offering. But Charity saw, for the briefest of instances, a covetous glint in his hooded eyes. Shohanno was not immune to the rich beauty of that bit of fabric.

Gallo saw it too. With many flourishes, like a magician manipulating his scarves, he folded the bright stream of red.

"This is for you, chief. A gift to show you the friendship of El Gallo, a friendship that grows tall and strong like the great pine trees in the heart of your mountains."

The Mexican extended his arms, the folded cloth lying across his plump, hairy hands.

Abruptly, Charity understood the nature of the moment. The sense of tension, of climax, hung heavily in the air. Gallo and his little band of thieves were at the mercy of the Apaches. Shohanno had only to nod his head and his warriors, limited in number though they were, would have not only the crimson slash of cloth but everything else the Comancheros possessed.

At last, the Apache chieftain reached out and took the cloth. Charity realized she had been holding her breath.

Gallo's smile became once more a smile of flesh rather than of stone. With a quick glance, he signaled two of his men and Charity realized those two were still on their horses at a little distance from the others, with their rifles resting across their saddles. El Gallo was no fool. He had kept a small trump up his sleeve in case Shohanno forgot they were friends.

There was a festive air about the gathering then. From the depths of the panniers lashed to the back of the pack mule the Mexicans drew forth more pieces of cloth—although none so striking as the gift that Shohanno had accepted—pouches of colored beads, tobacco, a looking glass, and bits of metal from which a small piece of granite and a great amount of patience could produce deadly arrowheads.

Charity and her mother sat on a rock and watched. After a time, Martha Phike said, "They seem almost like"—she searched for the word—"people."

"Who do you mean?" asked her daughter.

"The Indians, of course. They're nothing but animals, but when they're resting like this they seem, well, more human."

Charity shook her head.

"I don't know who's worse. The Apaches or the Comancheros."

Martha Phike frowned.

"Those others. They are nothing but bandits, I guess. But at least they act like human beings. They live in houses and wear clothes and . . ."

She paused.

"They're *civilized*. That's what I mean."

Martha Phike would have abundant cause to ponder the truth of that statement before the sun set on that very day.

Chapter Eighteen

A short distance away, in the shade of a gnarled piñon tree, the chief of the little band of Apaches and the fat bandit leader had begun their bartering, a process as cautious and complex as the sparring of a pair of gamecocks.

Gallo's hands were extended outward in a gesture of helplessness. He shook his head.

"I have no horses to spare, chief." He waved his hand in a short arc. "You see that I have only enough horses for my own men. And such horses. They are poor and weak from too much riding. They are not fit for the warriors of Shohanno."

Shohanno knew as well as did the Mexican that the little mountain-bred ponies had the agility of goats and the endurance of wild burros, but he only grunted.

"You have a pack mule. You let Shohanno have a horse. One of your men can ride the mule."

Gallo did not alter his smile.

"Ah, but the times when we must ride fast—those are the times we must have horses."

The bandit leader felt himself being crowded into a corner. His smile grew even broader.

"The Apache chief wants to trade, but what has he to offer?"

He gestured again at the little aggregation of Indians.

"Gallo sees nothing of great value in the hands of your people, chief. Your weapons are old. You have no hides or pelts with which to barter."

He paused.

"Ah, maybe it is that you have the yellow metal to trade. No?"

Shohanno shook his head, his long, black hair rip-

154

pling about his face. He had never understood the white eyes' devotion to the yellow metal that had to be grubbed from the earth like burrowing beetles. What he needed were more horses.

"The fat one is right," said he at last. "We have little to trade."

Gallo waited for the Apache to continue but Shohanno closed his lips and was silent. The Mexican was beginning to wish he had not approached Shohanno's band on this day. It was not going to be a profitable encounter.

It was his move and he delayed it as long as possible. But Shohanno's silence grew heavier, more menacing, by the moment.

At last Gallo said, "The white women. Two of them. Shohanno's fortunes have not been all bad."

It was the point the two had been sidestepping from the outset of their bartering. Shohanno was pleased that it was not he who had broached the subject.

Gallo's grin faded.

"Ah, it is too bad, though," he said, sighing.

The Apache looked quickly at the other man.

"Strange words come from the fat one's tongue," he said, frowning.

Gallo held out his hands in his peculiar gesture of defenselessness.

"*Sí*. It is too bad about the women. A man with no more than one eye can see they will not make strong workers. Together they will be less than one Apache squaw."

He took the stem of grass from his mouth and pointed toward the two women.

"The old one? She is not worth a man's breath to talk about." He stabbed the stem of grass toward Charity Phike. "You think the young one will make a good slave for the Apaches' lodge? I tell you, chief, I know these gringo women, the young ones."

He shook his head.

"*Trabajo?* Work? Of that they know nothing. This one. She would last perhaps a moon. No! A handful of sunrises doing squaw's work, and she would die. Like that!''

He slapped his leg with the quirt, but his words brought only a grunt from Shohanno. El Gallo was making barter talk.

After a time, the Apache said, ''The young one there. She is not so hard to look at. She would bring much gold to the pouch of El Gallo.''

The Mexican gestured deprecatingly.

''Ah. Perhaps. But it is a great distance to such a market in Mexico.'' He licked at the sore on his lip. The glint in his eyes was all the evidence Shohanno needed.

He sat in silence until Gallo shrugged and continued.

''*Quien sabe?* She might be of some small value to El Gallo. For her...'' He paused, as though giving his answer great consideration. ''For this grasshopper of a woman I will give the great Chief Shohanno five pounds''—he held up five stubby, widespread fingers—''of gun powder.''

Shohanno made no reply.

''And lead, much lead, for bullets,'' added Gallo.

The Apache chieftain made no acknowledgment of the Rooster's offer, but kept his dark, hooded eyes on the distant depths of the huge canyon. He waited so long to speak, in fact, that the Mexican began to feel beads of sweat appear on his forehead. Of a certainty, this would not be a good day for him.

But Shohanno spoke at last.

''Three horses,'' were the words he uttered.

Despite himself, Gallo breathed a breath of relief. At least they were still in the talking stage.

''The chief places great value on the white eyes.'' He leaned a hand's breadth nearer the Indian. ''For the young one I give Shohanno all the plunder I have named plus a measure of whiskey as well.''

He leaned back to watch the effect on the Apache. He was not disappointed. The dark eyes of the chief opened wider for an instant, then returned to their inscrutable squint.

"These things and a horse and mule," grunted Shohanno.

"What you ask is not possible, chief. One horse is worth three times this many women of the white eyes."

At this, Shohanno turned and fixed his gaze on the Mexican bandit. It was the gaze of a great eagle swooping down to snatch up a rabbit in its talons. Gallo had the sudden sensation he was standing on the edge of a very high precipice with the ground crumbling beneath him. If he was to salvage anything from this exchange he would need all the wits a lifetime of knavery could produce.

"The great Apache war chief is a terrible and courageous fighter. His name is spoken with fear and trembling by his enemies," he said in a somber tone. "But is the mighty Shohanno willing to make a wager in this matter? Is he fearless enough to gamble? The young woman against all the goods I have named—the whiskey and the gunpowder and other fine gifts your eyes have seen."

It was a thin thread to which the Mexican clung, but the Apache love for gambling was a truth not to be denied. Gallo held his breath.

"No! Those things already belong to Shohanno." He struck his bare chest with a clinched fist. "We gamble so: the woman for one of El Gallo's horses."

The Rooster ground his teeth but he kept his voice carefully even.

"Ah, the Apache chief drives a hard bargain. Of a certainty, Shohanno and his people shall have the gunpowder and tobacco and whiskey. From the beginning, these things were intended as gifts for my friends, the Apaches," he lied. "But El Gallo would be throwing away the life of one of his men to give up a horse. Would Shohanno do such a thing to one of his braves?"

Before the Indian could speak, the Rooster went on quickly, "Of course he wouldn't. Shohanno and El Gallo are both too smart for that. I will make this offer to the great war chief of the Mescalero Apaches. The woman for this fine mule of mine."

"And," he hurried on, "Shohanno may decide the manner of game to be played."

The bandit leader slapped his leg with his quirt and grinned confidently, a confidence he did not feel. But it was a chance he could not pass up. In the right market, deep in Mexico, the young gringo woman would fetch a handsome price, enough gold to buy a score of horses.

Quickly, too quickly, Shohanno gave his answer. Gallo, intent on the prospects regarding his own fate, failed to detect the warning tone.

"Let it be so," said the Apache.

He stooped and from the rocky hillside picked up a small stone no larger than a pellet of black powder. He put his hands behind his back, then held them before him, fists closed.

"Seven times you will make a choice. If you choose the hand holding the stone four times of the seven, the woman will be yours. If you fail . . ." He shrugged.

Not quite knowing why, El Gallo was glad the Apache did not finish the sentence.

In a matter of moments, members of Shohanno's band had moved in and formed a circle around their leader and the bandit chief. This was an occasion of some magnitude; a rare bit of entertainment in an otherwise Spartan existence.

Charity and her mother were left alone, sitting on the great slab of stone some distance away.

"Charity," said Martha Phike, wetting her lips. "What do you think they're doing?"

"I don't know, mama," answered Charity. "Making some sort of trade, I guess. I can't imagine what the game is that those two are playing."

"Well, I suppose it doesn't really concern us," said Martha Phike. "I'm just glad for the chance to rest."

Over in the center of the gathering of Indian warriors, old bucks, young squaws, and old, the leader of the bandits was wiping at the sweat that rolled from his forehead and stung his eyes. Three times he had tapped one of the hands extended to him and three times he had found nothing in the palm when Shohanno rolled his fist over and opened his fingers. Was it possible that the Indian had simply dropped the pebble and was offering El Gallo two empty fists from which to choose?

The Apache stood before him with outstretched hands balled into fists. Gallo's throat was terribly dry. He needed a drink, a drink stronger than the lukewarm water in his canteen.

He looked closely into the hooded eyes of Shohanno, hoping to find a clue. But he found only the dark, unfathomable depths he had tried previously to penetrate, without success.

He put it off as long as he could. Then, with perspiration oozing from deep creases of flesh about his neck, he reached out and tapped a hand. Slowly, very slowly, the Apache chief turned his hand over and opened his fingers.

There was the stone. The explosion of breath from the Rooster's throat was audible to every pair of ears in the semicircle of redskinned people.

Twice more Gallo tapped a hand, and twice more he was rewarded with the stone. Suddenly, the game was even, three and three. The Rooster felt his confidence slipping again. This was the moment of truth. This play would determine whether El Gallo went away poorer by a mule load of trade goods, plus the mule; or wealthier by a young woman he could sell for *mucho dinero*, or keep for his own pleasure, if he chose.

He studied the dark brown fists held out to him, hoping against hope to find something there that would give him a clue. The long interval passed in silence. Shohanno's patience was inexhaustible.

At last, Gallo reached out and, his stomach churning with misgiving, indicated a hand. Slowly, as slowly to Gallo as the turning of an aspen leaf from green to autumn gold, the Indian rotated the hand and opened his fingers.

Like a precious gem, the stone lay in his palm!

For a moment the face of Shohanno and his tribe and the mountains and the azure sky swam before the Rooster's eyes. He had won.

With a trembling hand he withdrew a sack of strong tobacco from a vest pocket and extended the pouch toward Shohanno. The Apache accepted it, made himself a smoke, and returned the sack to Gallo. After twice spilling the tobacco on the ground, the bandit leader fashioned a cigarette and guided the end of it toward his dust-dry lips.

Then Shohanno nodded. It was almost a smile that played on his lips.

"*Ussen* has smiled on the Rooster," spoke Shohanno. "The woman is yours."

Gallo's breast filled with rejoicing. He would count this day among his more fortunate ones.

"*Vamonos, hombres!*" cried Gallo to his men.

Quickly they emptied the panniers and saddlebags of the goods not already unloaded, and within a minute were mounted and ready to ride.

But during that short interval there had been quick, almost silent movement by Shohanno and a half-dozen of his warriors. The Apache chieftain stood beside the two captives. His braves had drifted outward and now formed a half-concealed perimeter about the steep, rocky hillside where the others were gathered.

El Gallo, however, was still counting his chickens and failed to notice. He rode to the boulder where Shohanno and the two women stood.

"Chief," he said. "It has been a good day for bartering. Both of us have profited from our meeting."

He turned and the smile faded from his lips.

"You," he said to Charity. "Get up here on my horse, behind me."

Shohanno's arm cleaved the air like the blade of a scimitar.

"No!" he said coldly. "It is not the young one you shall have, but the other."

Understanding burst on Gallo like the sun of a new day. This accursed Apache was trying to cheat him out of his treasure. He cast his gaze quickly about, gauging the position of his men. But what he saw made his heart rise into his throat. He and his men were effectively surrounded by Shohanno's warriors.

Through taut lips he asked, "Is the mighty Apache war chief going back on his word? We gambled for the young one."

The Indian stood with his arms folded across his chest.

"El Gallo listened to his own tongue. Shohanno said nothing about gaming for the young white eyes."

His face became a mask of stone.

"Now take your prize and go."

Gallo considered the several things he wanted to say, but at last he swallowed them, grimacing at their bitterness.

"Let's go," he said, the spirit drained from his voice.

Cruelly, he gouged the sides of his pony with his spurs and rode away, up the steep mountain slope.

The next three Comancheros followed, none looking at the women.

Charity held her breath.

But the fifth bandit rode beside the boulder and pointed a long, grimy-nailed finger at Martha Phike.

"You come," he said.

"No!" shouted Charity. "You can't take her. She is old and weak. I will go! Take me!"

But the bandit uncoiled his long, horsehair rope, tossed a loop over the head of Martha Phike, and let it drop to her waist. Then he took a dally with the rope, reined his horse about, and rode away up the hillside on the trail of his departing companions.

Charity hid her face in her hands and cried, afraid to see. But at last she could no longer bear it. She looked through her fingers, and the tears that welled from her eyes, and saw her mother trying to stay on her feet against the pull of the rope and the steep slope of the canyon wall.

When she fell for the tenth time, El Gallo rode back down the incline, cut the air twice with his braided rawhide quirt, then leaned down and slashed the buttocks of Martha Phike. The thin mountain air carried her screams to her daughter's ears.

Chapter Nineteen

Billy Joe Chance was off his horse again and kneeling down for a closer look at the marks on the trail. The canyon up which he and Arlo Smith had been toiling on this second morning was almost sheer rock. The marks of hooves, when they could be discerned on the limestone ledges, were indistinct scratches and scrapes. Chance felt the urgency gnawing at him as the sun slanted higher and their quarry multiplied the distance between them.

Chance got to his feet and swung back into his saddle.

"Can't do it," he said to the older cowboy. "That bunch could be plumb to Arizona by the time we put their trail together. Only way we'll have a prayer of catchin' up is to think like an Apache and ride like hell."

"I got a better idea," muttered Arlo Smith.

"Yeah? What's that?" inquired Chance.

"Let's think like a couple o' cowpokes that ain't gone plumb loco and turn around and ride back to the herd. If we're unlucky enough to catch up with that bunch of Apaches, we'll wish to heck we'd never got this bright idea." He paused. "We? What in tarnation am I sayin'? You're the one that got us started on this fool trail."

Arlo expected a quick answer but Billy Joe built himself a cigarette, pulled the drawstring with his teeth, and slid the sack of Bull Durham back into his vest pocket before replying.

"Maybe you're right, Smitty," he said thoughtfully. "I've got no business dragging you into this mess. It's my fault if it's anybody's. Tell you what. You head on back to the herd. Whitey needs lookin' after, anyway."

"What're you sayin', kid? You want me to ride away

162

and leave you to chouse them Injuns by yourself?" Arlo Smith demanded incredulously. "You talk like you've been bit by a hydraphoby polecat."

"I mean it," said Chance. "If I hadn't jumped in the middle of Will Phike about causing that stampede, he and his family would still be with the herd."

He pulled his hat down tight.

"It's my doin'. You ride on back. I'll pry those women loose from the Apaches. If they're alive."

Arlo Smith sent a stream of brown juice against a boulder jutting from the wall of the canyon.

"Chance," he said gently.

"Yeah?"

"Don't listen to me. I talk too much. Let's get to ridin'."

He gigged his horse into a struggling lope up the narrow trail.

They rode the trail hard until the sun stood straight above them. They had climbed until cactus and sagebrush gave way to scrub piñon and occasional junipers. In the lead, on the blood bay horse he called Catamount, Billy Joe pulled up suddenly.

"Look here, Smitty," he said, pointing. "Somebody came on the trail here and then rode back up the hill. What do you say we take a look?"

"Why not?" Arlo Smith shrugged. "Them's the first surefire tracks we've seen for quite a spell."

The two riders reined up the slope, up the steep hill where El Gallo and his four followers had led pudgy Martha Phike at the end of a horsehair reata. They topped out at the crest of the ridge and saw that the trail turned and climbed higher, toward the peak of the shale-mantled mountain.

With a high wind knifing at them, Chance and Smith pushed their horses hard, climbing for a time, then dropping down into a deep, rugged canyon before scrambling up its far slope. Where the canyon wall broke over, they stopped to let their horses blow. Arlo Smith, digging for the plug of tobacco in his pocket, let his horse drift off the trail. Billy Joe, glancing down, saw on a flat stone a mark that seemed strangely out-of-place.

Swinging down, he dropped to one knee and looked more closely at the stain on the rock.

"By gosh, it looks like blood," he said. "Blood from someone's bare foot."

"Billy Joe!"

The voice of Arlo Smith, oddly strained, came to Chance on the wind.

"Hold on," he shouted in answer. "There's blood on this rock."

"Billy Joe. Come here!"

The urgency in Arlo Smith's tone was unmistakable. Chance sprang into the saddle and rode the fifty paces to where Smith still sat his saddle.

"What is it?" Billy Joe demanded as he rode up.

Smith said nothing. Chance followed his gaze to an object a few yards away.

"Ah." Billy Joe let the breath escape from his lungs. "Who is it?"

"The old woman. The Phike woman."

Billy Joe dismounted, took a couple of steps, and then stopped. There was no doubt. It was Martha Phike there on the ground before him. She was lying face down, her buttocks propped up by a broken-over century plant stalk. Most of her clothes had been ripped from her body.

Billy Joe started to turn away, then looked back. Across Martha Phike's buttocks and thighs were a score of swollen, purplish welts left by a rawhide quirt. A large stone, stained with blood, lay beside her head.

Chance wiped his mouth with the back of a hand and slowly remounted the red bay horse.

"You know what, Billy Joe?" asked Arlo Smith. "They threw her away. That's what them damned Injuns did. They just threw her away."

After a time, Chance shook his head.

"I don't think so, Smitty. I don't think it was the Indians."

"Why not?" demanded Smith.

"This just isn't the way they do things. Not a bunch with squaws and kids along. Huh-uh."

"Well, you tell me who else would've done it," said Arlo Smith angrily.

"I don't know. Comancheros, maybe," said Billy Joe. "Did you see those gouges on her legs. Spur marks, I'd bet."

He shook his head again.

"Naw, this isn't the work of Indians. I'd bet a sawbuck on it."

"Well," said Smith, sliding the shotgun from the boot at his knee. "There's one way to find out. The trail heads off that way."

It was less than an hour later that they rode over a hogback ridge and saw the cluster of horses and, a few steps away, a handful of men gathered around a campfire built in the lee of a stone outcropping. They reined up quickly but one of the men at the campfire had seen them. He was pointing their way with the half-eaten leg of a jackrabbit.

"What do we do now, Mr. Trail Boss?" asked Arlo Smith.

Chance levered open the breech of his rifle to check the load, then shrugged.

"Don't appear that we have much choice. They've already spotted us."

"Think them's the ones?" inquired Smith.

Billy Joe jerked the dirty red and white neckerchief from about his neck and knotted it around the barrel of the .44–40 rifle.

"I'd bet a month's wages on it," he grunted.

The two cowboys rode side by side down the slope toward the cluster of Comancheros. There was a single picture in the minds of both: the ravaged, tormented body of Martha Phike, thrown aside like a worn-out boot.

Four of the five men around the campfire had drifted out from the rocks where they had been positioned as the two riders approached. El Gallo, though, kept his place by the smoky fire and watched the horsemen ride toward them. Through his mind was running a quick stream of possibilities: either the two riders were mighty brave or they were *muy stupido* to ride into El Gallo's camp. If it weren't for the rag tied to the gun barrel, he'd already have given the order to empty those two saddles. But Gallo was a curious man. He would find out what the two strangers had on their minds before he blew out their lights.

Billy Joe's gaze took in the positions of the five men as he and Arlo Smith rode slowly forward. Two of the bandits were standing together a distance from the fire, another was leaning against the off side of the rock ledge against which the fire smoldered, and a fourth was standing beside the horses.

Those were the followers, Chance mused. That would be their leader standing beside the fire, his foot propped up on a rock and a cigarillo hanging from his lips.

They pulled up ten paces from the fat man with the sore on his lip.

"Howdy," said Chance, letting the rifle drop until it rested across the swell of his saddle.

"Buenos tardes," said Gallo. "What you two *hombres* doing out here in these badlands? Huh?"

Billy Joe grinned a broad, sheepish grin.

"Me and my pardner here have got ourselves lost," he said. "We're with a trail herd drivin' up the Pecos. Thought we'd scare us up a deer and have some fresh meat. But ..."

He let the sentence die and shook his head, still wearing the hangdog expression.

The grin remained on El Gallo's face but his eyes were narrow slits.

"Sure," he said. "I understand. You two get down off those horses and have some coffee. Then I'll tell you how to get back to the river. Hokay?"

Billy Joe sent a quick glance to Arlo Smith, then made a motion to dismount. But suddenly he stopped and settled back in the saddle.

"Say, amigo," he said to the fat Mexican. "We come on to a funny thing on the far side of that ridge. Seen a body." He laughed, a cold, hard laugh. "Wasn't hardly anything left but some coyote bait."

It was the laugh that put the Mexican off guard. That, and the fact that these two greenhorns weren't going to leave his campsite alive.

"*Sí*." His grin split the sore on his lip again. "We made us a little trade with some Apaches. That old woman cost me a good mule."

He slapped his leg with the quirt that hung around his wrist.

"Should have kept the mule. That *vieja* sure didn't last long."

The barrel of Billy Joe's rifle was resting carelessly across his saddle. The muzzle was centered on El Gallo's breast bone.

Billy Joe shot a quick glance at Arlo Smith.

"Are you ready?"

"Anytime." Smith nodded.

Suddenly, comprehension came to El Gallo. He knew then that he should have followed his first impulse and killed the two strangers when they rode within rifle shot. But comprehension was late in coming by a heartbeat or so.

As the Rooster's hand descended to the six-gun on his hip, Billy Joe thumbed back the hammer on the rifle in front of him and pulled the trigger. He had time to consider that he hadn't given the Mexican much of a chance. And he didn't really care.

The bandit leader was slammed backward. He fell squarely across the campfire, but appeared to take no notice.

Billy Joe was vaguely aware of two thunderous explosions, one on the heels of the other, as he jacked another round into the rifle's breech.

He swung the rifle barrel in a short arc and pulled the trigger a second time. The bandit standing beside the big boulder managed to get off one shot with his pistol. The slug whistled past Billy Joe's ear as the bandit slumped against the boulder and slid to the ground.

Chance looked quickly at Arlo Smith. He was reloading the double-barreled shotgun. Twenty paces in front of him lay two more of the Comancheros, victims of a double load of buckshot.

But where was the fifth man? Chance's gaze made a quick inspection of the rough terrain the bandits had chosen for their campsite.

"Where's that other *hombre*?" demanded Chance.

"Beat's me," said Smith. "Maybe he took off. . . ." He stopped. "No, there he is. T'other side of the horses."

Billy Joe jerked the rifle to his shoulder. All he could see of the man were his feet and legs beneath the belly of a tethered horse. He snapped a shot that missed the foot of the hidden bandit by a scant few inches. Instantly, the man behind the horse leaped into view. His hands were held high above his head.

Holding the muzzle of the rifle on the man's midsection, Billy Joe spurred the blood bay toward him.

"Don't shoot, señor. *Por favor.*"

The voice was that of a youth. Drawing closer, Chance saw he was, indeed, young. And he was mortally afraid that another moment would be his last.

"Step out here," ordered Billy Joe.

"No, señor. Don't shoot me. I beg you."

The youth came around the horse's head and fell to his knees.

"Get up," said Chance. "Where's your gun?"

Fearful that any move toward the gun would bring a quick end to his tender years, the young bandit stretched out a toe and kicked the gun from beneath the horse. Billy Joe had to suppress a grin. The pistol was an ancient navy Colt .36—unlikely, from its appearance, to cast a bullet at any predetermined point on the compass.

"How old are you?" snapped Chance.

The Mexican looked down and scratched a collection of small stones into a heap with the unstitched edge of his boot.

"Diez y ocho," he murmured.

Chance heard Arlo Smith chuckle.

"If this yahoo is eighteen years old, I'm a hundred." Smith rode up beside Billy Joe. "We're wastin' time we don't have to waste. Let's get to movin'."

"Keep your shirt on," said Chance.

He swung the muzzle of his rifle squarely at the boy's midsection.

"I need a couple of answers."

"Ah, señor. Anything you ask I will tell you truthfully." Billy Joe's gaze was unswerving.

"Tell me about the women."

"It was El Gallo. He traded with the Apaches."

"Where's the other gringo woman?"

The cocking of the hammer on Billy Joe's Winchester was a singularly unpleasant omen in the thin mountain air.

"She is alive! On my father's grave I tell you this." The young bandit dropped back to one knee. "She is with the Apaches." He waved an arm toward the towering Guadalupe Mountains.

"We're wastin' a mess of time," said Arlo Smith.

Chance frowned at him and turned back to the youth.

"What were the Indians figuring on doing with the woman? How many braves and how many squaws were in the bunch? Which way were they headed?"

As Billy Joe finished the questions he let the muzzle of his rifle find the youth's chest again.

"And I want the straight of it. Hear?"

"Sí, señor," said the youth, shaking his head vigorously up and down. "The Indians were going up the cañón grande. The big canyon that leads to their grounds high up there."

He waved with a quick hand.

"I would say Shohanno had this many braves." He held out both hands but curled under a couple of fingers.

"Horses?"

"Not so many horses. Even some of the old warriors had to walk."

"Why didn't Shohanno take your horses?"

The youth, feeling a reprieve in the atmosphere, shrugged eloquently.

"They played a game. El Gallo won. He thought to take the young woman, too. But all he got was the old woman. And it cost him his pack mule."

The lad shrugged again.

"As for what Shohanno is going to do with the

woman, I cannot guess. I think he was going to make a gift of her to one of the old warriors.''

Arlo Smith swore.

''Billy Joe, dang it! Let's get to ridin'. I say we let some daylight through this mangy little coyote so's he can't do us no harm before we get goin'.''

''Shut up a minute,'' snapped Billy Joe.

To the youth he said, ''You interested in joining your friends here or do you think you can find your way out of these mountains by yourself?''

The boy's eyes grew wide.

''Ah, señor. You are a thousand times too kind and merciful to this ant of a human being. If you let me go I will never look back and I will be thankful for the rest of my days that you came this way.''

Chance jerked a thumb toward the smoldering campfire.

''Well then, grab that jackrabbit that's fried to a cinder and head out across those mountains yonder.'' He gestured northward. ''And don't bother to pick up a gun or anything else you might have a hankering for. I've about run out of patience.''

The teen-age would-be bandit wasted no more breath on time or words. He rolled the scorching body of El Gallo out of the cinders, grabbed the blackened jackrabbit, and, with almost the same loping gait as a jackrabbit, disappeared over the crest of the hill.

''Huh!'' snorted Arlo Smith. ''That's a mistake.''

Chance was silent. That made it worse for Smith.

''When you take a notion to let your straw boss in on whatever is floatin' around in your head, just don't be bashful about speakin' right out. Hear?''

Finally, Billy Joe spoke.

''I've got an idea. Probably get us both killed. But we can't ride off and leave that Phike girl to the whims of Shohanno and his bunch.''

Arlo Smith shook his head.

''You're right as rain, Chance. We cain't do that. So let's you and me run down that bunch of Injuns and make sure all three of us get our scalps peeled.''

Chance ignored the sarcasm.

"The way I see it, ol' Shohanno wants horses a heap more than anything else. So let's see if we can help him out."

He swung his hand in a quick arc.

"Let's get these extra horses unsaddled. Pronto!"

Arlo Smith uttered a halfhearted oath.

"I can see there ain't no reasoning with the likes of you when you've got your head set."

In a matter of minutes they had the Comancheros' horses unsaddled and tied neck-to-neck. All except the tough little mustang that the bandit chief himself had ridden. At Billy Joe's insistence, Smith left that horse saddled and bridled.

"I hope you know what we're doing," said Smith.

"Bait," said Billy Joe. "We're going fishing and these here cayuses are what we're using for bait."

Arlo Smith rolled his eyes heavenward.

"Why, dagnab me! Anybody in his right mind should ought to have seen that." He spat a stream of tobacco-hued liquid and muttered, "Now, how in tarnation could a growed man like me allow hisself to be drug up here in these mountains by a half-witted kid?"

"Let's get to movin'," said Billy Joe suddenly.

They reined away in a lope, heading to an intersection with the trail up which Shohanno and his people were moving. Behind them lay the scattered corpses of the Rooster and his henchmen, all except a youthful member who would wake in a cold sweat many a night to come because of the vividly frightening events of this day.

It was rough trailing and hard on the horses, but an urgency was eating at Billy Joe that kept him pushing forward. The blood bay horse he had inherited from the dying Comanche brave half a lifetime ago was equal to the task.

They caught sight of the Indians sooner than they had expected. Almost too soon. They crested a bald, rocky ridge and instantly saw the collection of Apaches moving up the game trail that paralleled the floor of the canyon. They were a half-mile, no more, from Shohanno's band.

Billy Joe waved Arlo Smith back and spun his own

horse about, hoping no sharp-eyed Apache had happened to glance their way. Luck was with them. There was no untoward movement among the Indians.

Arlo Smith grunted and swore.

"Now, ain't we the lucky ones? Why don't you ride on down there and explain to that Apache what you have in mind, Chance? I'd kinda like to know myself."

Billy Joe grinned a tight grin.

"Well, you bein' your usual sweet self and all, I'll let you in on it."

He gestured toward the far side of the canyon.

"Those Indians want horses worse than anything, including scalps, is my guess. So I'm going to give 'em something to occupy their time while you and me have us a game of cat and mouse plucking that little gal out of their midst."

Arlo Smith mumbled under his breath again. "Half-wit" was one of the milder epithets that issued from his lips.

Chance was pointing again.

"See that brushy ravine cuttin' through the bottom of the canyon? I want you to take these four horses those Comancheros were kind enough to give us and head 'em down the far side of that ravine. In a dead run. What I hope to do is get ol' Shohanno and all his mounted braves to take in after them. And while they're playin' roundup, you and me will grab the girl. . . ."

Arlo Smith bumped the heel of his hand against his forehead and groaned.

"I liked it a heap better when I didn't know what you was plannin'."

Billy Joe glanced skyward.

"The sun won't wait, pardner. It's time we made our move."

They eased away from the hogback ridge. Guarding cautiously against being seen by the Indians, they drifted down toward the floor of the big canyon until they were safely shielded from any chance gaze by an Apache.

"Give me ten minutes to get in close to the squaws, then you head those ponies down that canyon like a bat out

of hell," said Chance. "And try to stay out of sight while
you're doing it."

"You're a big help. Yeah, you are," said Smith.
"Whatever happened to the simple little ol' trail drive me
and you was makin'?"

Leading El Gallo's wiry little brown horse, Billy Joe
started a circuitous route that would, he hoped, bring him
close to the band of Indians moving at a walk up the trail.
He had had a quick glimpse of Charity Phike and the
manner in which she was moving and he feared she would
be of small help when it came time to make a run for it.

It began to look easy. Too easy, Chance thought. If
the Indians wanted horses as badly as he hoped they did,
his simple little scheme would work like the well-greased
hub of a wagon wheel.

Shohanno and his mounted braves were leading the
band of Mescalero Apaches along the ascending trail. It
was slow movement, what with more than half the party
made up of squaws and kids afoot. Billy Joe didn't think
Shohanno would be charitably disposed toward anyone
who might fall into their path.

It was at that instant that the storm broke. Billy Joe
barely had time to reach the point on the mountainside for
which he was aiming when a long, shrill cry broke from
the throats of a half-dozen of the Indians. They had seen
the horses!

Shohanno wasted no time in unnecessary conjecture
about his good fortune. With a bronzed, sinewy arm
holding his rifle above his head, he shouted commands and
kicked his pony into a dead run. Every warrior on horseback followed suit. It left only Stone Belly behind with the
squaws, but that venerable warrior had ideas of his own.
He stripped the panniers from the pack mule in an instant,
swung onto the animal's back, and was quickly caught up
in the dust cloud that rose behind the other riders.

Billy Joe quickly scanned the lower reaches of the big
canyon. Arlo Smith had done his job well. He had stayed
hidden while sending the four Comanchero ponies racing
through the thicket-choked canyon floor.

It was all the opportunity Chance wanted. He burst

over the ridge into the midst of the band of Apache squaws and children.

"Charity Phike!" he bellowed.

The girl looked around her in astonishment. Even as he rode closer, she seemed not to understand what was happening. She shrank from him as if he were a total stranger, a hostile one.

"Get in the saddle!" Chance ordered.

Dazed, she obeyed, but it seemed to Billy Joe she was moving in quicksand.

The Apache squaws were hardly less dumbfounded. They stood and watched Charity climb laboriously into the saddle on the mustang.

"Hold on!" shouted Billy Joe to Charity, and, wheeling, he gigged his horse with a mighty stab of the spurs. It was almost too much for Charity. Despite her hold on the big Mexican saddle horn, she swayed and came perilously close to tumbling to the rocky hillside.

The departing braves were oblivious to Chance's actions, however. Stumbling onto a band of horses, even a paltry handful such as these, constituted more good fortune than they had encountered in all their wanderings of the past two weeks. Would an old fox like Shohanno let such luck as this slip through his grasp? Hardly.

Down the steep, narrow trail went Chance. Once he looked back, and then he kept his eyes ahead. Charity Phike was not at home in a saddle and the glance he had of her, tilted far to one side on the pony, sent a wave of apprehension through him.

Ah, but there was Arlo Smith ahead, just coming back to the trail. Billy Joe uttered a small prayer of thanksgiving that something, at least, was going right. He began to feel a confidence that up to now had been little more than false hope.

It was the hawklike vision of the aging Stone Belly that gave them away. The old Apache, riding the mule and far to the rear of his companions, saw the three riders and bellowed a warning that could be heard a half-mile up and down the canyon. Instantly, Shohanno divided his forces, some continuing on the trail of the stampeding mustangs, the others falling back to give chase to the two men and the woman.

"Our luck just ran out!" Chance shouted to Arlo Smith.

"Tell me about it," replied Smith. "My scalp sure don't feel like it's stuck on very tight right now."

Despite the urgent need for distance, Billy Joe pulled his horse back until he was beside the girl.

"You going to make it?"

Tears streamed down her face, but she nodded.

"I'm all right," she said, her voice choked. "Let's just get away from here."

She started to say something else. All Billy Joe heard was "Mama?" He knew what the question would be and he didn't feel like dealing with it at that moment.

So the three of them headed down the precipitous trail with their horses running full out. Shohanno and four of his warriors were closing the distance with a speed that warned Billy Joe their opportunity for flight was pinching down to a sliver of time.

The westering sun was sliding toward the horizon and Billy Joe knew the Apaches would make every effort to corner their quarry before dark. The Apaches believed that he who kills in darkness must spend his eternity walking about in darkness.

The Indians were almost within rifle range. A fortuitous shot could even now destroy what they had so painstakingly schemed. Billy Joe heard one shot from a big-bore rifle but then they were turning a hairpin corner on the trail and were out of sight of the onrushing Indians.

There was a moon, although little enough light for hard riding on that trail. But Billy Joe knew it was one big roll of the dice now. They would have to push their horses to their limits, ride them to death, if necessary, in order to reach the herd where they could call on the drovers to stand off the Apaches.

He figured the herd would have reached the Bosque Grande some fifty miles south of Fort Sumner by this time. If he misjudged that rendezvous, it would be a case of Katie-bar-the-door. Shohanno still had a big score to settle with the trail herd. He had come in peace to barter for horses—until Whitey O'Bannon had blown his segundo from the back of his horse with no more compassion that he would have felt shooting a rabbit.

The question of the fate of Charity Phike's mother couldn't be hidden forever. The first time Billy Joe called a halt to let the horses blow, Charity asked it.

"Do you know what happened to mama?"

Billy Joe hesitated. Would a lie help? Probably not.

"She didn't make it. I'm sorry," he said. "The Comancheros . . ."

He listened to her sobs for a time. Then she said, "Mama thought the Indians weren't as civilized."

Chance didn't pursue the subject. He didn't want this girl to know what had become of her mother. Not right at that moment, anyway.

Arlo Smith was uncharacteristically silent. Chance looked at him in the quicksilver of mountain moonlight.

"What's on your mind, straw boss?" he inquired. "Can we afford to give these ol' ponies a rest?"

He was surprised at the answer.

"You're the stud duck. You make them heavy decisions."

Chance shrugged.

"Okay. Let's rest 'em a couple of hours. Daylight's not that far away."

He added, "I'll keep an eye peeled. You two get some rest."

Smith made no reply, but stepped down from his horse, loosened his cinch, and lay back against a down-slanting boulder. It seemed only an instant to Billy Joe before he heard snoring drifting from beneath the hat that covered Arlo Smith's face.

Billy Joe unrolled his slicker from its place behind his saddle and spread it on the ground for the girl.

"Sorry about your family," he said, then couldn't decide what to add. But the girl only shook her head.

"I was afraid it would turn out like this. I tried to tell pa."

Chapter Twenty

The first timid tendrils of daylight came quickly. Chance rose.

"Better get to moving, Smitty," he said. But he had to say it twice more before Arlo Smith stirred. Then Billy Joe understood. The one rifle shot he'd heard the evening before when they had begun their flight from the Apaches had found a target. Arlo Smith had taken a rifle bullet below his left shoulder blade. The fact that he had been able to stay in the saddle for most of the night was indisputable testimony to the indomitable nature of the old man's constitution.

Abruptly, Charity was kneeling beside him. She looked into the ashen face of Arlo Smith and then up at Billy Joe. The question burned there, unspoken.

Arlo Smith saw it, too.

"Hey," he said, putting on a lopsided grin to mask the pain. "This ain't nothin' but a little ol' scratch, honey. I've got myself hurt worse than this nailin' shoes on a horse."

But then he turned his face away and she couldn't see into his eyes.

Chance unbuttoned the old man's shirt, turned it back for no longer than a slow, painful moment, then pulled it closed again.

"Can you get on a horse?"

"I'll be ridin' when you're hobblin' around on a walkin' stick," said Arlo Smith, some of the old fire back in his tone.

He had to have help to mount, though. But once in the saddle on the little strawberry roan horse he was at

177

home again. In the uncertain light of the false dawn they headed down the trail.

In a strained voice, Smith asked a question.

"How long before we reach the herd?"

"If they're where they should be we ought to strike 'em at that big bunch of trees they call Bosque Grande," said Billy Joe. "I'd judge it to be a couple of hours away. We can't afford to drag our feet."

Almost as one, the three riders turned and scanned the higher reaches of the canyon behind them. No riders were in sight.

But, in the next instant, they saw a flash of movement in the junipers and Billy Joe knew they had cut it too closely. The Apaches had closed to within a frighteningly short distance while they had rested there on the mountain.

"Let's go!" he shouted, and whipped the rump of Charity's horse with his reins. Away they flew down that little game trail, their horses sliding on the shale and sending stones flying out into space to fall a hundred feet before striking ground again.

The shooting started, but even an Apache warrior had to have some luck to hit a whipping, dodging target a half-mile away.

Billy Joe saw the big clump of trees and shouted the news to the girl and Arlo Smith. They were going to make it after all!

Their horses were tired. Fatigue caused them to stumble and falter but Chance drove them on, raking the blood bay with his spurs, slashing the hindquarters of Charity's mustang, and shouting at Arlo Smith to spur ahead.

The trail became less precipitous as they neared the river. Brush-choked ravines and eroded gulleys became their enemies.

Billy Joe wanted every drover with a gun ready to turn back the Apaches. He pulled his six-gun and fired into the air and drew instant response. Every member of the trail herd from the cook to the wrangler was instantly armed and ready.

It was not an easy crossing of the Pecos River there, but the urgency of the moment put that hazard low on the list of priorities. Their horses were into the stream and swimming frantically for the opposite bank.

It was not a long, drawn-out battle. Shohanno was nobody's fool. He had had a bellyful of drovers and in a matter of minutes had signaled his warriors to retreat. They vanished up the mountain trail almost as quickly as they had stampeded down it.

The punchers gathered round Billy Joe and Arlo Smith and the girl named Charity and were oddly silent, not knowing what to ask, not sure they wanted to know the details of the trio's experiences.

It was Solomon who opened the subject.

"You're crazier than a bedbug, both of you punchers. Don't you know them Apaches don't forget. I wouldn't be surprised if they rounded up a hundred other bucks and come a-callin' on us again."

He swore under his breath.

"And besides that, somebody run off with my scattergun. Was that you, Smith?"

Billy Joe was jerked suddenly back to his senses. Arlo Smith was a badly wounded man and needed attention. The gnat's whisker by which they had eluded Shohanno's warriors had caused him momentarily to forget that dread fact.

With unaccustomed gentleness, the drovers lifted Arlo Smith from his saddle and laid him on the sand in the shade of the chuck wagon. It was Charity Phike who took charge. She cut his shirt away, exposing a great, blood-blackened wound in his back. There wasn't much that could be done with it, Billy Joe knew. Stop the bleeding and hope for the best.

Chance looked into the eyes of Arlo Smith and bit his lip.

"You'll make it, old-timer," he said.

"Among your other faults, you ain't much of a liar," replied Smith.

Chance got to his feet.

"Where's Whitey?"

"Yonder he comes," said Solomon.

Then he added, "That Whitey has had hisself a lot of fun pushing the herd and issuing orders to these here cowpokes. To tell you the truth, I figger he figgered you boys would never come out of the mountains alive. He was all set to drive these longhorns plumb to Fort Sumner and hog all the credit.''

Billy Joe watched Whitey ride up and he was surprised at the cold feeling that reached from his hat brim to his boot heels. Whitey was his old self: cocky, arrogant, ready to take on anyone or anything. He stepped down from his horse.

"Never figured to see you *hombres* again. For that matter, there wasn't no need to. I've got this old trail herd eatin' out of my hand.''

Billy Joe had made up his mind. The wound in Arlo Smith's back had settled it. The Chance-O'Bannon feud wasn't quite dead. It had to have one more offering.

"Whitey, it's going to be me and you now,'' he said in a quiet voice. "And it's not that old feud that's going to cause it. I just want you to know that. It's the fact that you played the fool when you shot Shohanno's brave out of his saddle and set off a war that's cost a half-dozen lives, maybe more.''

His voice was husky.

"Is that clear enough?''

It caught Whitey by surprise.

"What the hell are you sayin'?''

"You've been wanting a showdown ever since I joined this outfit. Well, I'm telling you that time has come.''

Whitey threw back his head and laughed.

"That's just a jim-dandy idea, Mr. Chance,'' he said, chuckling. "I'll take this herd on up the trail after I've shown you how an O'Bannon handles a pup named Chance.''

He backed away.

"Anytime you're ready.''

Billy Joe hadn't expected Whitey O'Bannon to crawl or try to deal his way out of the showdown. There was nothing in his makeup to suggest cowardice. He was a confident man with confidence in his ability to kill his own snakes.

The drovers faded out and back, away from the line of fire. Billy Joe looked down at Arlo Smith lying in the shade of the wagon and knew it was the right thing to do. The debt Whitey owed had grown considerably greater than simply another round of lead in something called the Chance-O'Bannon feud.

There was no signal spoken, and none needed. The two cowboys, thirty paces apart, drew and fired. The gunshots sounded as one. Billy Joe felt the bullet tear into his thigh. The ex-straw boss had got off his shot and he was still standing, waiting for his adversary to fall.

But then Whitey rose on his toes, and stretched himself backward until it seemed he was trying to fold himself in half. Then he fell to the sandy bank of the Pecos and lay still.

Charity Phike screamed but it was a brief, shocked scream that went nowhere. Slowly, the drovers moved forward. They fidgeted and looked down at the man they had ridden with and then looked off into the distance.

Not yet feeling the pain of the bullet in his thigh, Billy Joe knelt beside Arlo Smith.

"That was for you, pardner."

Arlo Smith licked his lips. His voice was dry and cracked.

"Thanks a heap." He motioned with his hand. "I shore could use a swig of that there water in your canteen, Mr. Chance."

Billy Joe withdrew the stopper, lifted Arlo Smith's head from the sand, and held the mouth of the canteen to his lips.

Smith's eyes were growing glazed again. He started to take a swallow of water, but then the haze that clouded his eyes lifted suddenly.

"Where'd you fill that canteen?" he mumbled.

"The river," answered Chance.

Arlo Smith sighed a long, tired sigh and weakly pushed the mouth of the canteen aside.

"If it's all the same with you, Billy Joe Chance, I think I'll just pass. Cashin' in is bad enough. I don't see no reason why a man ought to make it worse with a swaller of that Pecos River water."

He started to grin but the grin didn't quite make. Arlo Smith closed his eyes there in the shade of the partly burned chuck wagon on a bald, sandy knob of prairie that sort of leaned out over a hairpin bend in the treacherous, serpentine course of the Pecos River.

ABOUT THE AUTHOR

Writing Westerns is, for me, a natural reaction to the Southwest's infinite blue skies and majestic mountain-desert landscape, the kind of country that spawned a special breed of men: bold and self-reliant, rawhide tough, and bighearted to a fault. If you look closely, you can find traces of those qualities even today among the oldtimers who inhabit New Mexico, the setting for *Bitter Pecos*.

New Mexico was also the setting for my boyhood, years spent hunting, fishing, exploring on horseback, and helping wrest a living from land that was more hostile than fertile.

Following an unremarkable performance in high school, I enlisted in the Navy in time to catch the final act of the Korean conflict, serving as a radar operator aboard an amphibious assault ship.

After a four-year hitch, I returned to New Mexico and enrolled at Eastern New Mexico University, ultimately earning a bachelor's degree in journalism and a master's in political science.

Newspapering has been my life's work since. I've had stints on dailies in Texas, New Mexico, and Kansas, and for the past decade I have served as managing editor of the Clovis *News-Journal* situated at the heart of New Mexico's High Plains region and an hour's drive from the site where Sheriff Pat Garrett fed Billy the Kid Bonney a fatal dose of lead barely one hundred years ago.

I grew up in a world of Westerns. On my tenth Christmas, I was suffering from a head and neck injury caused by a spill from a horse and I was supposed to be resting my eyes. Therefore, I had to hide in a closet because I was so eager to read my gift—one of Graham M. Dean's juvenile Westerns. Years later I worked for the old gentleman, as editor of a newspaper he owned.

I read most of the great Western writers: Zane Grey, Max Brand, Luke Short, Clarence Mulford, Ernest Haycox and, in later years, that master of Western story-telling, Louis L'Amour. For a youngster whose earliest ambition was to become a cowboy, they provided a wealth of enjoyment and, quite probably, the seeds of a yen for writing.

Such were the stepping stones that led me to write my first novel, *Season of Vengeance*. In it I have tried to give readers a picture of that New Mexico about which I spoke, of the men and women who tamed it, and of those who died trying. I was needless to say very proud when it was selected as the winner of the Bantam Books / Twentieth Century Fox First Western Novel Contest in 1981.

I then set to work on *A Reckoning at Arrowhead*, a second novel set in the New Mexico Territory of the 1800s, a time when cattlemen fought renegade Indians, merciless elements, and sometimes each other, to build their empires. *Bitter Pecos* followed soon thereafter, and I'm now at work on my fourth book.

Despite a degree of bondage to a typewriter, I make time for my wife and three children, and an ornery gelding that regularly forgets he's broke to ride.

W. W. SOUTHARD
Clovis, New Mexico